The SECOND CLONE

Other Scholastic books by Carol Matas:

Cloning Miranda
The War Within
Rebecca
Lisa
Jesper
Daniel's Story
After the War
The Garden
In My Enemy's House
Greater than Angels
Of Two Minds (with Perry Nodelman)
More Minds (with Perry Nodelman)
The Lost Locket

Carol Matas

Cover art by Ginette Beaulieu

Scholastic Canada Ltd.

Toronto New York London Auckland Sydney
Mexico City New Delhi Hong Kong

Scholastic Canada Ltd.
175 Hillmount Road, Markham, Ontario L6C 1Z7, Canada
Scholastic Inc.
555 Broadway, New York, NY 10012, USA
Scholastic Australia Pty Limited
PO Box 579, Gosford, NSW 2250, Australia
Scholastic New Zealand Limited
Private Bag 94407, Greenmount, Auckland, New Zealand
Scholastic Ltd.
Villiers House, Clarendon Avenue, Leamington Spa,
Warwickshire CV32 5PR, UK

National Library of Canada Cataloguing in Publication Data

Matas, Carol, 1949-
The second clone

ISBN 0-439-98813-6

I. Title.

PS8576.A7994S42 2001 jC813'.54 C2001-930477-3
PZ7.M37Se 2001

6 5 4 3 2 1 Printed in Canada 01 02 03 04

For Diane Kerner,
one of a kind!

Chapter 1

Every morning when I wake up it's the same thing. Slowly I surface from a wonderful dream. Emma and I are performing together on Broadway. I'm dancing. She's singing. And then the singing turns into the songbirds outside my window. I breathe in the scent of lemons and roses before my eyes even open, and I'm happy.

Then I remember. I'm the first human clone.

* * *

"Miranda!"

I sit up, the dream gone. Ariel is standing over me, hands on hips. "Are we not going?"

"What time is it?"

"9:03. Late. Very late. We must train ourselves to rise early. On Monday we return to school."

"You train yourself," I retort grumpily, pulling the covers over my face.

"I *am* trained," she points out. "I am up and ready."

"Then you mean I must train *myself*," I correct her, turning over, talking into the pillow.

"I suppose."

"Well, I don't need to be trained. I know how to go to school. I've never been late. You're the one who's never done it."

"Yes. I am a novice, as you say," Ariel agrees.

I yearn for the peace and quiet I enjoyed before Ariel moved in with us. But, I remind myself, it was all my idea, having her move in. And now I should be nice to her. After all, as weird as this is for me, it must be even weirder for her. Raised in a lab. Never been outside before she came to live with us. Cloned from me as nothing more than substitute organs should any of mine fail. And when mine did fail, instead of allowing her to die, to sacrifice herself for me as she'd been brought up to do, I go and insist that she live. And come home with me. And be my sister. And it *has* only been three weeks since we got home from the clinic, which used to be her home.

I flip over on my side away from Ariel, and run my hand over the slightly raised scar across my abdomen where they cut me open and gave me half of Ariel's liver. All the pain is gone now. In fact, as I lie here, I realize that I pretty much feel completely normal, the way I did before I first got sick.

"I am full of anticipation," Ariel says.

"Are you still there?" I ask.

"Of course."

I sigh. Well, I asked for it. And I'm just going to have to get used to it. I propel myself out of bed and head for the bathroom.

"I'll be ready in fifteen minutes," I say. "What's it like out?"

"We are situated on a twenty-acre farm, three miles from the city limits," she answers. "It is a very attractive property, palm trees marking the boundaries. A long bungalow sits in its centre. Landscaped . . ."

I am holding in a giggle but I can't hold it for much longer.

" . . . with a mixture of grapefruit, lemon and orange trees, Madagascar palms, aloe trees and *Senita cereus* or whisker cactus. An extensive cactus garden is situated around the house, including *Opuntia* or prickly pear, *Mammillaria magnimamma* . . . "

"Ariel."

"Yes?"

I can't help but laugh a *little*. "When someone says 'What's it like out?' they want to know the weather, not a description of the environment."

"Then why do they not ask, 'What is the weather like?' " Ariel demands, her cheeks getting pink.

"It's an expression," I explain. "You'll have to get used to it."

"Yes," she says. "You are correct. I want to be more like you."

"How much more like me can you be? You're my clone! Try to be more like yourself."

She gives me a puzzled look.

"Oh, it's way too early for this," I say with a sigh.

I go into my bathroom and shut the door. At least here I can have privacy — well, now that I've made it clear to Ariel, who is sharing my room, that she may not enter while I'm in here. I thought it would be easier for her to adjust if she initially bunked in with me, rather than being in one of the guest rooms. And after some prodding, Mother agreed to let her design one of the guest rooms for her own. She's chosen all reds and greens and yellows: bright, vibrant colours. I suppose they're delightful to her after the monotony of the lab. Today's shopping trip is also part of my effort to help her be herself.

We start school Monday and I think she should choose her own clothes. Right now she only has the ones Mother bought for her. Besides, after being stuck in this house with her for three weeks, this is a great excuse to get out of here for an afternoon.

I go into the kitchen. Lorna has made me a breakfast of fresh grapefruit, a mushroom omelette and toast.

"Would you like to eat it here or outside, Miranda?" she asks.

"Where's Ariel?"

"She is outside, on the patio."

"I'd better join her then."

We have a number of patios. Lorna is pointing to the one outside the kitchen. There is also one off the dining room which looks over the pool and tennis court and one off my parents' room. I like the kitchen patio best. It's surrounded by cacti, and some of them always seem to be in bloom. I join Ariel outside, helping Lorna carry my plates. Ariel's face brightens when she sees me.

"Do we leave soon?"

"Yes," I answer. "As soon as I've eaten I'll tell Mother we're ready."

"I have been thinking about Mother," Ariel says.

Uh-oh. There is no such thing, it seems, as

a relaxed morning breakfast where we chat about what we might want to shop for at the mall.

"Emma is meeting us there," I say, trying to distract her.

"Excellent. Now about Mother." She pauses. "She really is not my mother," she states. She pauses again. "Or yours. My mother is you, as I am cloned from you. And your mother is the child you were cloned from."

"No," I object, "not really. You are more like my twin, only four years younger, and I am like a twin to the original one, Jessica, their child. So Mother really *is* my Mother, and yours, because she and Father had Jessica. If Mother had cloned herself," I say, "and you were the result, *then* you would not be her child but her twin. You and I are sisters."

"Of course," she sighs with relief. "You are correct. As always."

"Well, Dr. Mullen engineered extra smarts into you as well as me," I say. "So I'm sure you are just as clever as I am. You just don't know enough yet."

"But today I will learn about The Mall! I cannot wait!"

"Then let me eat," I declare.

She finally shuts up and lets me eat. I eat slowly, which I know she finds maddening, and when I'm done I go in search of Mother.

She is busy on the phone as usual, probably with one of her charities.

"Ready?" I mouth.

She nods and waves. Now that I know how old she really is, she seems to have aged before my eyes. After all, she had me after Jessica died, and Jessica was already ten. Now I'm fourteen, and so instead of being thirty-five like I thought, she's actually in her early fifties. The miracles of plastic surgery. But they can't cover the worry lines she's developed since I almost died, and since I started hating her. Well, maybe that's too strong a word. But I still haven't forgiven her or Father for what they've done.

She gets off the phone and smiles. "You girls all ready for your first day out?"

"We are," I say.

"Take a sweater in case the mall is over-air-conditioned," she says, like she always does before I go to the mall.

"I don't need one," I remind her, like I always do, except now I know why — I'm genetically engineered to have a perfect blood flow and I'm almost never cold. Another little "advantage" Dr. Mullen gave me. Also superior healing abilities, or I'd never have gotten well as fast as I did after the surgery and the treatments.

She nods and doesn't argue with me like she used to before the truth came out. In fact, our relationship is nothing at all like it was before I learned the truth. We used to be close. Now she behaves as if nothing has happened, as if somehow I'll just forget how they lied to me about my entire life. I take a deep breath. Just looking at her can set me off and get me angry all over again.

It's only a twenty-minute drive to the mall. I convince Mother to put the top down on her Mercedes convertible and I revel in the hot air blowing in my face. The boulevards are a mass of flowers, the sky is blue and I'm happy to be alive. Mother screeches up to the front of the mall. "Two hours," she says.

"Three," I demand. "We can't do everything in two."

"Fine," she sighs. She can't seem to argue with me anymore. Sometimes it feels like I'm the mother. And I don't like it. I want to be an innocent kid again. But I guess those days are over.

Emma is already waiting at the main entrance. She's a sight for sore eyes. I'm used to seeing her every day at school and talking on the phone just isn't the same. She's been over at the house a couple of times since the surgery, but it's not like hanging out on our own away from all parents. We give each other a big hug. She hugs Ariel too, who doesn't really understand she's supposed to hug back.

"What do we do first?" I ask.

"I guess we give Ariel the grand tour," Emma says. "Come on."

So we begin with a walk up and down the mall, showing Ariel the stores, what people buy in them, all that. Ariel is full of questions.

"But why do people need to purchase beauty products? Can you create beauty like that?"

Emma laughs. "No! And mostly we know that, but we fall for it anyway."

"Fall for it?" Ariel says.

"Yeah," grins Emma. "We know it's not true but we let ourselves be convinced. Just in case, I guess."

"Not logical," Ariel states.

At this point we get to a See's Candies store.

"Shall we?" I say.

"Of course," says Emma.

We go in. There's a long line and when it's our turn, I'm ready with my choice, a chocolate truffle. Emma picks a chocolate cream, but Ariel has no idea what to choose. She questions the salesperson about each chocolate, pointing and saying, "And what exactly is that one?" Behind us the crowd is getting restless.

"Give her a soft caramel," I finally say to the person serving us, a young girl who is starting to look at Ariel as if she's an alien. I mean, who doesn't know what chocolate is all about?

We take our treats out into the mall and eat them right away. When Ariel bites into hers, she says through a full mouth, "I understand *this*. This makes more sense than beauty products. I would pay dollars for *this*."

"Come on," I say. "Time to shop."

We take her into the department store.

"There is so much," she declares.

"Yeah, isn't it great?" Emma says. "Oh! Look at that, Miranda." And she rushes over to a rack of new summer tops, obviously just in. A rack of bathing suits catches my eye. I'd like a one-piece this season, not a bikini, so my scar won't show.

I am still looking through them when Emma comes up to me and says, "Where's Ariel?"

I whirl around. "I don't know. Just figured

she was following us. Ariel," I call, peering around the racks of clothes. "Ariel?"

Emma starts calling too, but Ariel is nowhere around.

"What do we do?" I say, panicked. "She has no idea about anything! I should have warned her to stay close. She's no smarter than a two-year-old about the outside world. She could go off with a stranger, or — or anything!"

"A stranger won't know she's not streetwise," Emma reminded me. "She's somewhere. Don't worry."

"We should split up," I suggest.

"Okay. We'll meet in ten minutes," Emma says. "You go look for her. I'll alert security and get her paged. We'll meet at the security desk in the centre of the mall."

I hurry off, not knowing where to look first. In the store, out in the mall . . . I rush up and down the aisles, asking salespeople if they've seen a girl who looks like me, blonde, blue eyes, but younger, tall for her age, which is ten . . . No luck. I hear the announcement. "Will Ariel Coburn please report to the security kiosk in the centre of the mall." And then a description of exactly where the security kiosk is. That was smart of Emma.

I have no luck in Macy's so I hurry out into

the mall, over toward security. I see Emma. And then I see Ariel heading over there, too.

"Ariel!" I exclaim, running over to her, not knowing whether to hug her or rebuke her. "Where did you go?"

"Go?"

"You left me and Emma!"

"Is that incorrect?"

"Of course! You could have gotten lost."

"How? We are in an enclosed space."

"But a big space with lots of people. What if you'd been kidnapped!"

"Kidnapped? Abducted by an evil person?"

"Yes!"

"Why would anyone want to do such a thing?"

I look at Emma for help.

"There are lots of people in this world, Ariel," she says, "who *can* be trusted. Almost everyone. But there are a few that can't. And we have to be careful. Just in case."

"That is sad," Ariel says.

"Yes," I agree. "But sadder if something bad happens to you. So from now on you stay with me when we're out. Always. Understand?"

"Yes. I understand."

"Good."

Emma looks at her watch. "We'd better

help Ariel," she says, "or we'll leave here with nothing for her to wear on her first day at school."

"I enjoyed hearing my name called all over this structure," Ariel says as we walk.

I shake my head. What am I going to do with her?

Chapter 2

I wake up every morning now vowing to have more patience with Ariel. But within minutes I'm so mad at her I could kill her. It's been like this for the whole three weeks we've been back at school.

This morning, for example. I told Lorna I would wear my new grey shirt with my grey pants and black hooded sweater to school. Only my grey shirt was nowhere to be found. Well, it was finally found at the bottom of the dirty laundry basket. Why? Ariel wore it last night when she went out for pizza with her new friend Jen. And spilled tomato sauce on it. Tomato sauce! Honestly! I thought it would get better once we went to school and we weren't stuck at home together constantly.

And Emma doesn't understand. She says she'd love a little sister. That's only because she has two older brothers who boss her around all the time and she wants someone *she* can boss around. But I never get to boss Ariel around. I'm either looking after her or letting her walk all over me.

I am thinking all this as I wait for her to get ready so we can get to school. She flies into the kitchen and stuffs an entire pancake into her mouth in one go as I yell at her.

"You're impossible! We'll be late! Let's go!"

"So we'll be one minute late," she says, although I have no idea how she can talk with her mouth full like that. "So what?"

So what? I feel like I must have smoke coming out of my ears. "So what? So . . . we can't be late!"

She washes the pancake down with a giant glass of fresh-squeezed lemon juice — no sugar — then grins. "Ready!"

I shake my head and shudder. I can hardly watch her drink that every morning. Lorna was making her fresh lemonade one day when she grabbed it up before the sugar was added and declared it delicious. Now it's her favourite drink.

"Mother, we're ready," I call.

Mother hurries into the kitchen. "Where is your knapsack?" she says to Ariel.

"Here it is," Lorna says. The same thing every morning. Ariel forgets it, Lorna has it ready for her.

"And my grey shirt." I glare at her as we go out the door. The heat hits me, just like stepping into an oven, even though it's only seven-thirty in the morning. I stop for a moment and gasp. A May heat wave. The sky is blue and there are no clouds. The flowers Mother has planted all around the house are waiting patiently for their eight o'clock watering, when the sprinkler will turn on automatically. The lemon tree is heavy with lemons right now, and the huge cacti in the centre of the yard are unfazed by the heat, of course. I wish I could be like them. Tall, and stately, and strong. I used to be. Now Ariel has my stomach in a knot and my life turned upside-down half the time.

"My grey shirt?" I repeat, as we get into the car, top up, air conditioning on.

"I'm really sorry," Ariel blabs at a mile a minute. "But it was my first time out with Jen and her family and I wanted to make a good impression and you weren't here to ask and I was sure you'd want me to look good, it matched just right with my purple pants. And the purple top I got to go with them was too much, don't you think?"

I open my mouth to answer but she rattles on.

"And then I spilled on myself. I was so

embarrassed, I'm really sorry about the shirt, but who knows if they'll ever take me out again!" And she looks like she is going to cry.

"Of course they will," I find myself saying. "I mean, if Jen is a good friend she won't let a silly thing like that stop her."

"It's silly?" Ariel asks.

"Yes. Silly."

"So then you aren't mad about it?"

See? She's got me again! How can I be angry when I just told her it wasn't worth getting upset about? It's even more annoying that she's almost impossible to stay mad at. Even though I hate to admit it, because I am so ticked off right now, she's really adorable. She loves me to bits, which is kinda sweet, and she is so enthusiastic about absolutely everything that it's contagious. Things I take for granted, like fresh air, and candy, and new clothes — they are all marvels to her. Still, I have to start to draw the line with her occasionally, and this is a perfect opportunity. Can't have her stealing my clothes!

"It's different," I explain to her. "Jen won't think it's important because everyone has accidents. On the other hand, you took my shirt without asking. That's not an accident. So I can be mad. Understand?"

"Yes," she says formally, much more like her old self, "I understand."

I'm on a roll, so why stop now? "You have to grasp," I continue, "that I am your older sister. You need to listen to me. You need to ask my permission before you do things."

"Miranda!" Mother interrupts me.

"Well, Mother, this is getting out of control," I complain. "She needs to know I'm the boss."

"You are not the boss, dear. Ariel, your mother and your father are the ones you need to listen to."

"Not Miranda?" she says.

I glare at Mother.

"Well . . . " she hesitates. "Not in the same way. Naturally Miranda is full of good advice, and I would consider it in your best interest to listen to her."

"Thank you!" I say.

"But," Mother says, "in a family it is your parents who are the final authority." I am sure that Mother means that as much for me as for Ariel. She too, has noticed that I have been deciding what's best and maybe now she thinks it's time for her to be the mother again.

"I think I understand," Ariel says seriously. She pauses and I can almost hear her thinking. "Does anyone, then, ever have to listen to *me*?"

I laugh. "No! Because you're the youngest."

"She's teasing you, Ariel," Mother says. "Of course we will listen to you. That's part of being a good parent. We all must respect each other."

I decide to let that pass. Respect doesn't include telling your child the truth when the truth can put you in a bad light, I think bitterly. But I bite my tongue and say nothing.

"I will try harder to be a good sister," Ariel says. And she looks like she means it.

"Thank you!" I reply, and I suspect I have a smug look on my face because Mother glares at me.

"What?" I say innocently.

She shakes her head.

* * *

"It's amazing," I say to Emma when we are changing classes. "Ariel and I are from the same DNA. And yet she's so different."

"But she was brought up so differently," Emma points out. "And now that she's not in a lab anymore and she's experiencing freedom for the first time ever — well, freedom seems to be the thing she cares about most."

"Freedom to annoy me, you mean," I grumble

as we head down the corridor to math class.

"Maybe that's the only way she can make herself different from you," Emma says.

"Differentiate herself," I muse. "That makes sense, I suppose."

"It should cheer you up," Emma points out. "It means you are you, and she is she . . . or is that she is her? . . . "

We sit at our desks and instead of concentrating on class my mind begins to wander. What Emma said is true, I guess. Or is it? I don't know — ever since I discovered I'm a clone of Jessica, Mother and Father's first child, I've wondered who I am. Am I just a pre-programmed package, a copy? Do I have my own personality? Well, Ariel is a clone of me. And she seems to be very different. So maybe Emma *is* correct and it isn't all predetermined. Or maybe Ariel is just like me, but she is trying to be different.

And I suppose since we've only been at school three weeks since our recovery, she has had lots of adjusting to do. It's amazing that in this short time she has almost completely stopped speaking in that formal, stilted way. I think she's gone a bit overboard, trying to sound like all her classmates, but she's very bright and picks up speech patterns quickly. She also instinctively understands how important it is to fit in. And that's what she's been working on. After all, she was brought up in a lab with no other children. She was more like a lab rat than a child — so learning to socialize is her big job now.

And it's great that the middle school she attends is in the same complex as our high school. We share the same library and the same lunchroom, so I see her every day at lunch. She's learning quickly.

I shudder as I replay the scene in the principal's office when Mother and Father told the principal that Ariel was their niece. "She was raised by my sister," Mother said, looking like butter wouldn't melt in her mouth, "in an isolated research facility with no other children. And when my sister died unexpectedly, well, of course we took her in. We would appreciate you viewing her as Miranda's sister, not her cousin, as we are adopting her."

Mrs. Dean was terribly sympathetic. But it was all lies, more lies. And what I hated the most was seeing how good Mother was at lying. I don't see how I can ever trust her again. As we were leaving the office Mrs. Dean said, "But she could be her sister. She's the image of Miranda!" Image is right, I was tempted to say. She looks like that because she's my clone created by a mad scientist at my parents' request so that should I need any extra organs, she could give them to me and then die! Wonder how that would have gone over? Love to have seen the expression on Mrs. Dean's face then!

I try to put all these thoughts out of my mind and get down to work, but I can't stop thinking about Ariel. I shouldn't have yelled at her. After all, she gave me half her liver and saved my life. What's one ruined shirt in comparison? I'll apologize as soon as I see her.

"Miranda!"

I look up. Mr. Thomas is glaring at me. "Please pay attention! Exams in three weeks. And you have just missed a third of the term!"

"Yes sir," I say, wondering why I insisted on coming back to school.

Emma winks at me. She'd tried to convince me not to come back. "Are you crazy?" she'd said. "A chance to skip the rest of the year, and they'll give you your grades until now and no exams and you say *no*? It's that need-to-be-perfect thing, isn't it?"

But I want to get my grades the way everyone else does. I don't want to be any more different than I have to be.

After class we head for the lunchroom. As we are sitting down I see Ariel on the other side of the room. She is just standing there, staring around in a kind of daze. I wave and try to catch her attention, but she doesn't seem to see me. Then she walks off.

"Hang on," I say to Emma. "I'd better go talk to her. Maybe she's ignoring me because she's mad about this morning."

I hurry over to her as she is about to sit at a table by herself.

"Hey," I say.

She looks up. "Oh!" she exclaims. "Miranda!" She says it like she's surprised to see me.

"Weren't we going to meet for lunch?"

"Were we?" she says.

"Well, if you want to be that way, fine," I say, knowing perfectly well she hadn't forgotten. Every day she's made a fuss about eating with me and Emma and my other friends. I forget all about apologizing. "If you don't want to eat with us, don't," I say and I stalk off back to Emma.

Before she came into my life I didn't even know I had a temper. Now she looks at me the wrong way and I get mad. I glance back over my shoulder to see her sitting there all cool, as if she hadn't just blown me off.

She's obviously mad at me about how hard I was on her earlier. I suppose I'll have to make it up to her. I sigh with frustration as I sit down beside Emma. "Remind me again how lucky I am to have a sister," I say.

Chapter 3

Today after school Ariel is coming to ballet lessons for the first time, and I'm having my first class back since my illness. The recital was a huge success, and most kids are finished for the year. But those of us who are really serious about dance usually take the spring/summer session. Mother is picking Ariel and me up right after school. I say goodbye to Emma and see Ariel already waiting by the school drive. It's the first time in two weeks that she's been there before me.

"Hello, Miranda," she says. She smiles. Maybe she isn't mad after all. That would be good. Maybe that little talk with her had the desired effect and I don't have to apologize.

"Well, hello, Ariel," I say in response.

Silence.

"How was your day?" I ask.

For the last three weeks I haven't had a chance to ask. She's just blurted everything out at a mile a minute.

"My day was fine," Ariel says. "I attended French class but found the work difficult."

"Well, you'll catch up," I assure her. "I mean, you're starting at the end of the year after all, and I don't know why you wanted to start with something as hard as a new language, anyway. You can always drop it, no one will care. You aren't taking exams anyway."

I expect her to contradict me and to insist that she can do anything — Mother and Father didn't even want her to go to school until next year but she said if I was going, she was going! Instead of her usual spunky answer she nods her head and says, "Perhaps I should quit, as you suggest."

I look at her, stunned, but have no chance to reply because Mother squeals up and motions for us to jump in.

"Ready for your first ballet class, Ariel?" she asks.

"Yes," Ariel replies. "I am interested in everything. Everything is new and interesting." But she doesn't look excited, and yet yesterday it was all she could talk about. She must be really mad at me, really upset. Still, I have no intention of giving Mother the satisfaction of seeing me apologize so I decide to talk to her later.

When we arrive at the dance studio I let Mother take charge of Ariel and I go to my first class. Mr. Lovejoy is teaching this session. He is a retired dancer from the Arizona Dance Theatre, and is the real thing. I've heard he won't take any nonsense. And did I hear right! He puts us through our paces like he's a drill sergeant. "Taller, taller." He comes up and sticks his finger in my back. "Get that head up! Bum tucked in. Arms extended! Extended!" And this is just in the *pliés.* By the time the class is over I know I won't even have to wait until the morning to be sore. I'm already sore! And drenched in sweat. But it's great to challenge my muscles and I note that I don't feel weak, a good sign. My scar doesn't hurt either, also a good sign.

"An excellent beginning, boys and girls," he says, clapping his hands. "But from now on we work! Yes?"

I practically stagger out. I can't wait to get home and shower. But I am dying to hear how Ariel liked her class. As soon as we are in the car I ask her, "So? How was it?"

"Interesting," she answers.

"Just interesting?" I say, disappointed. "But you were so excited. Is anything wrong?

"Why?" she seems worried. "Is something wrong with what I am doing?"

"No, no," I assure her. "You're just so . . . I don't know. This morning you were so keen. You sound different now. Did something happen?"

"I thought you *wanted* her to be different," Mother interjected. "Make up your mind, Miranda. You gave her a big lecture this morning. She's obviously just trying to please you."

"Is that it?" I ask Ariel.

"Yes, I am trying to please you. Of course. That is my reason."

I sigh. So she *is* mad. Or overreacting in some mammoth way. "I'm sorry, Ariel," I say. "I didn't mean to upset you this morning. Just forget what I said. And remember that I am not your reason for living. You have to find your own reason."

"Well, Miranda," Mother says, "you say that, but you don't really mean it. As soon as she acts like herself you say that she's annoying."

"I don't wish to be annoying," Ariel says. "I wish to please."

I am really confused now. Of course this is just what I wanted, but somehow it seems too weird. Why the sudden turnabout? She didn't sound like she had any intention of listening this morning. Could there be some bizarre programming engineered into her that she *has* to listen to me?

She is in the back seat and I am up front with Mother. In a low voice I say to Mother, "Did Dr. Mullen program her in any way I should know about? Why is she reacting this way?"

"I'm sure he didn't, Miranda," Mother says. "Probably she is just trying to find her place with you. Perhaps she feels she went too far and now she's decided to be more compliant."

"You mean she's trying out different personalities?"

"Yes. Something like that. She has no idea yet who she really is."

I feel terrible. I was obviously way too hard on her this morning. On the bright side, if Mother is right, this version of Ariel could be far more accommodating than the last one. Maybe I should encourage her, not discourage her. It could work out that she'll be an excellent little sister, if she can keep this up.

As soon as we get home I take a long hot shower and as the water runs over me I start to feel bad. I mean, how selfish can you get? I can't keep Ariel down just so my life is easier.

Father is already at the table when I drag my aching body to the dining room. "Hello,

Miranda," he smiles. "I hear you have a new ballet teacher."

"More like sadist," I groan, as I sit down.

"Well," Father says, "you are getting to a very high level now. Many of the others in your class are thinking of a career in dance. Are you sure you want to keep it up?"

"Of course I'm sure!" I say, forgetting about Ariel for the moment as she sits eating quietly. "And who knows, I may want some sort of a career like that myself." I take a deep breath. It's now or never. "In fact, I want to talk to you about acting classes. Emma and I have found a very good new school and we want to take classes together."

Mother and Father both say "No!" at the same time.

"We've been over this, Miranda," Father says. "This is California. Every child takes acting lessons. Every kid wants to be a movie star. And every kid *can* be. That's how much talent it takes." He pauses. "You're special. You know you are. You have an exceptional mind. You can be a research scientist, a doctor, something that could change people's lives."

"As if science is the only thing worthy of me," I scoff.

Ariel is sitting quietly, looking interested. I

turn to her. "And don't think this doesn't involve you! They'll have the same rules for you too, you know."

"But they are the parents," Ariel says. "They decide."

"Aah!" I scream, throwing down my napkin. "Forget everything I said to you this morning. They can't decide everything!"

"They cannot?"

"No!"

"Why?"

"Because . . . because some things we have to decide for ourselves." I glare at my parents. "I never questioned you before. But things are different now. I have to make my own decisions. And I don't want to be a movie actor, anyway."

"That's a relief," Mother says.

"I want to be on Broadway!" I announce. "And I know I'm a good dancer. But the chorus line is all I'll be able to do if I can't act too. And sing."

"But you can sing," Father says.

"Of course I can. I can do everything! Why give me all these talents if you never wanted me to use them?"

This shuts them up. Because they know it's true. They had Dr. Mullen alter my genes to give me extra abilities — athletic talent and intelligence. The thing is, I don't know about the acting. It's one of the things it seems Dr. Mullen didn't know how to program for. I don't even know if I can do it. And that's why I want to try.

"Maybe it'll be something I can call my own — not something I was programmed for."

Just then Lorna comes in with the phone. "Ariel, it's your friend Jen."

"My friend?" Ariel says. "Do I have a friend?"

"Ariel," I scold her, "you've made a friend, be nice to her."

She looks at me for a moment and then says, "If you say so." Lorna hands her the phone, which she takes. She listens, then holds the phone away from her ear and frowns at me. "She wants to go to a movie together Saturday." She looks confused.

"Say you'll go," I tell her.

"Yes," says Ariel, then hands the phone back to Lorna. A bit abrupt, I think, normally she'd babble on and Mother would have to tell her it's rude to talk at the table. But I need to press my point with my parents.

"So, can I go?" I ask.

"No," Father reiterates. "I understand what you are saying, Miranda, but you'll thank us one day for saving you from this choice. You are meant for better things."

This is whole new territory for me. Until I discovered what they'd been up to I thought I had absolutely perfect parents. I would never have dreamed of going against them, because I wouldn't want to worry them and I assumed that they knew best. Now Father keeps wanting to "talk" but I'm not interested — still, it's at least better than Mother's attempts to pretend nothing has happened. I try to think what to do next. I need lessons from Emma on fighting with your parents.

"You're being a snob," I say to Father, unable to come up with anything else. "Why is theatre less worthy than science? Don't the arts make our society what it is? Isn't that important?"

"Of course," Father says, "but let someone else do it. You have other talents."

"You don't know what my talents are and neither do I," I fume. "But," I say under my breath, "I'll find out."

I can see he isn't going to budge so I eat my dinner in silence, then leave the table. I have to phone Emma. This isn't finished. Not by a long shot!

Chapter 4

I call Emma as soon as I get to my room.

"Emma," I say, keeping my voice low, "they wouldn't go for it."

"I told you your plan would never work," Emma says.

"I had to try the honesty thing first," I insist.

"Okay. You tried. And it didn't work. Of course."

Emma has this double standard about honesty. She's really a very honest person, except where her parents are concerned. With them, if they don't agree with her, well, she just goes ahead and does as she pleases anyway. And lies if she has to. The thing is, her parents are so reasonable that, although she always says she does as she pleases, she rarely has to go against them. When she does, it's mostly things like staying out till ten-thirty instead of ten.

"So now it's Plan B," Emma says. "You stop

trying to convince them and just do what you want."

"What will our cover story be?" I ask.

"Well," she answers, "Mom and Dad know I'm going. They've even agreed to pay for the classes."

"Lucky I'm so frugal," I say. "After all those years of saving my allowance, I've got enough money to pay for years of acting classes."

"Right, then," Emma says. "The new session starts this week. So let's do it." She pauses to think. "I'm just not sure how you'll get away with it. Your parents know what you're doing every moment of the day."

"Why can't I just say I'm coming over to your house after school?" I ask.

Emma laughs. I can almost see her shaking her head. "Boy, are you green at this. They are bound to phone here and the first thing my mom will say is that we're at drama class. No, you have to do better than that. Let me think."

Ariel walks in.

"Gotta go. Talk later." I hang up.

Ariel looks around the room as if she's never been here before. She stares at me.

"What?" I ask.

"What?" she repeats.

"What are you standing there for?"

"What should I be doing?" she says.

"I don't know!" I exclaim. And I wonder to myself just which is more annoying — her not listening to me at all, or this new good-little-sister act. Then I have an idea. "Actually, there is something you can do for me."

"Yes?" she says eagerly.

"You can be my cover tomorrow."

"Cover?"

"Yeah, well, cover story."

"Cover story?"

"Yes. Can you keep a secret?"

"I don't know," she answers.

"Well, can you or can't you?" I say, exasperated.

"You tell me," she says.

"You can," I tell her.

She smiles. "Then yes, if you say I can, I can. A secret," she repeats. "Something that no one can know."

"Exactly!" I say. "Here's the deal. This drama school is located in the mall. I'll tell the parents I'm taking you shopping. You wander around the stores for an hour — if you promise not to talk to strangers — or wait for me in the lobby. We go home. And that's my cover story."

"Cover story?" she asks. "What is the secret?"

"The secret is I'm not going to be shopping, I'll be at an acting class. And you are my cover story."

"Will I be useful?" she asks.

Back to that. Born to serve me. "Yes," I sigh, "you'll be useful. Are you sure you are all right?"

"What do you think?" she asks.

I'm not sure if she is really asking me or being sarcastic.

"I'm not sure."

She stares patiently at me.

Well, I can't worry about her weirdness now. I have to get this plan sorted out. "So, will you do it?"

"I will be useful and it will be a good plan." She nods solemnly.

"Excellent," I say.

* * *

The next morning as we drive to school my stomach is full of butterflies.

"Mother," I say, "I've promised Ariel to take her shopping after school."

"Oh," Mother says, "but don't you want me to take you both?"

"No," I explain. "We, we need to bond. Can you drop us?" I ask. "And pick us up after?"

"All right," Mother agrees.

Then I have an inspiration. "Maybe we can

make it a weekly thing. You know, I'll take her for a soda or a piece of pie at Marie Callender's. What do you think?"

Mother beams at me. "I think it's lovely," she says.

I sit there in stunned silence. I can't believe how easy that was! And she has no idea. No idea at all.

Mother pats my hand. "What a good girl you are, Miranda," she says.

All right, now I feel guilty. But it wouldn't have come to this if they hadn't been so unreasonable. I mean it's not as if I'm asking if I can get a tattoo or stay out all night or anything. I've never touched a drug or had a drink! I *am* a good girl. I just want to take a silly acting class. If I'm ever a parent I vow never to be so stupid.

When we get to school Ariel stops for a minute as if to get her bearings and then heads off.

"So I'll see you after school," I remind her.

"Do we not meet at lunch?"

"Sure. I'll meet you for lunch," I agree. "It's just I thought you'd want to start spending your lunch period with Jen."

"Jen. My friend?" she says.

"Yes. Your friend." I shake my head. "Now get going."

Emma is waiting for me just inside the front door. "Have you come up with a plan?" she asks.

"Yes! And it's working like a charm." I tell her about it.

She looks at me admiringly. "Who knew? You've turned out to be a pro!"

"I don't like it," I say. "But they've left me no choice."

"You feel guilty," Emma says. "But don't. They shouldn't have been so stubborn. I'll tell my mom that I'm going on my own," she adds, "so if our parents ever talk they won't hear about it from my folks."

We are at our desks by now.

"Are you excited?"

"Am I ever!"

"I'm nervous," Emma says.

I love any new situation. Emma says I know no fear. I can hardly wait for school to be over.

Chapter 5

Mother drives us and cheerfully drops us off. The plan seems to be going like clockwork until Ariel and I walk into the mall. Suddenly Ariel grabs my hand, holding on so tight it hurts.

"What's the matter?" I say.

"Afraid," she replies.

I look at her, puzzled. How can she be frightened when she's a clone of me? Almost nothing scares me, certainly not walking into a mall. And anyway, she and I were just here with Emma and she loved it.

"What's scaring you?" I ask, concerned.

"Too many people. Too many things."

"It's a mall, isn't it?" I say, frustrated.

I hope there isn't something unexpected happening to her. Who knows with a clone — maybe the wiring in her brain has gone haywire. I don't like the thought of that. Could it happen to me, too? After all, if I'm the very first human clone and she's the second, well, no one really knows anything about us yet, do they? Maybe her brain has misfired or gotten scrambled or some strange thing. I've been reading all I can find on cloning, and one of the reasons so many scientists are against human cloning is because of all the things that can go wrong, and are going wrong, with animals that are cloned. When one cloned mouse turned the equivalent of thirty in human years it suddenly became horribly obese. Other clones were born with only one kidney, or blind. I mean, who knows what's in store for me and for Ariel in the future?

Ariel keeps a grip on my hand, an iron grip, and shrinks up against me like a monster is after her. She obviously isn't going to be wandering around on her own like I'd planned. She drags along after me, upstairs, to the space where the new drama school is. I register and pay my money. And then Emma turns up.

"I had trouble ditching my mom," she says. "She wanted to come up and register me but I was afraid she'd see you. Hi, Ariel. Aren't you going shopping?"

"No!" Ariel exclaims.

"She won't let go of me," I complain. I take Emma aside, telling Ariel to wait where she is. “Ariel is acting very strangely,” I whisper.

“How?”

“I’m not sure, just less like Ariel. More like she used to be.”

“Well, what do you expect?” Emma asks. “She was brought up, from the time she was a little baby, to give up her life for you. You saved her from that. But ten years of having ‘You were created to serve Miranda,’ drummed into her . . . think about it. When you got angry with her she probably really took it to heart.”

“Great,” I reply. “So now I won’t be able to say a word to her, no matter how annoying she gets.”

“Doesn’t sound to me like she’ll be getting annoying.” Emma points out. “She’s probably decided that she must be a good little sister at all costs. Even if it means not exploring who she really is.”

“But you know I don’t want that!” I say. “And what do I do with her now?”

“Maybe the teacher will let her stay and watch,” Emma suggests. She goes over to Ariel. “Would you like to come in with us?” she asks. “If you’re quiet,” she adds sternly.

“I will be very quiet,” Ariel agrees.

Emma registers. Then the girl who registered us points to a door. We walk in slowly, looking around. It is a large bare room with a few chairs at one end.

"Hello! I'm Tara, your teacher."

Tara has long, straight blonde hair streaked with grey. She's wearing a tie-dyed T-shirt and a long paisley skirt. Aging hippie, I think. Favourite music — Jefferson Airplane and Bob Dylan. But the great thing about old hippies is that they are very laid-back. She's quite happy to let Ariel stay and watch.

There are already three other kids standing around waiting — one of them a drop-dead gorgeous boy with curly black hair and blue eyes.

After we introduce ourselves, Tara starts us off with what she says is a standard acting exercise, mirrors. You get into pairs and you take turns copying each other's moves. Who do I get paired with? Dale, the gorgeous guy! I feel like I'm in a dream the whole time. I get to stare at him and it doesn't look like I'm staring because I'm supposed to.

After that we do a relaxation exercise on the floor. Then we do an exercise where Tara gives each of us a character — mine is a bored computer geek — and then she tells us we are at an office party. It is really funny!

The time flies by. When we're finished I go

over to Ariel, who has been sitting on a chair not moving a muscle.

"Come on," I say to her. "We have to hurry. We're meeting Mother in the shoe department at Macy's. Now don't forget," I say. "We've been shopping. The drama class is a secret."

"I will not forget," she says. And then I notice a tear trickling down her face.

Emma catches up with us as we're hurrying out the door.

"What's the matter, Ariel?" she says.

"I do not know," Ariel replies.

My heart sinks. Something *is* wrong with her.

"Why am I crying?" she asks.

"I don't know," I answer, getting more worried. Shouldn't she know? "Are you sad?"

She answers. "I am . . . I want to be where I am used to being."

"You want to go home?" I ask.

"Yes!"

"It's okay," I assure her. "Come on. We'll go find Mother."

Emma waves goodbye. "Call me," she says.

"I will."

I take Ariel to our meeting place with Mother, who is there waiting.

"So girls, did you have fun?"

"Ariel is a little upset," I say to her. "I think we'd better go home."

"What is it, Ariel?" Mother asks.

"I want to be back where I am used to everything. But I need to comply. I must serve Miranda."

Mother looks bewildered. "Ariel," she says, "you can go back to being the way you were before Miranda scolded you yesterday."

"Scolded?" Ariel says.

"Yes, don't you remember?"

"Miranda never does anything wrong," Ariel says.

Now I *have* to say something. "Ariel," I say, "I'm really sorry for yelling at you yesterday. I was just annoyed about my blouse. But it was stupid. You can go back to being yourself."

"Myself?"

"Like you were."

"Please tell me exactly how to be, and I will be that."

"But I can't tell you that!" I exclaim. "You have to find out who you are. But," I say in my own defense, "it's normal for sisters to fight, so I should be able to yell without you overreacting like this."

"You can yell," she says, "you can do anything. I am made for you."

I turn to Mother in frustration. "Mother,

there's something wrong with her! She doesn't even understand what I'm saying!"

"I think you might be right, Miranda," Mother agrees. "Something is off. We'll call Dr. Mullen to be on the safe side. He knows her best."

"Dr. Mullen will be angry," Ariel says, suddenly very alarmed.

"Don't be silly," Mother assures her. "Of course he won't. Come along, dear."

This child is a stranger to Mother really. She's been home with us for less than two months, and that's only because I forced Mother and Father to take her in. But I have no illusions. It's me they love. They are trying to be good to Ariel, but if she turns out to be defective or sick, they might not want to keep her. I have to wonder if what I said really has triggered this reaction in her, reminded her of the Prime Directive, so to speak. And I feel awful. Really, I love Ariel a lot. I was annoyed with her, but I didn't want her revert to her former behaviour!

We get home and Mother calls Dr. Mullen. Ariel sits in her room as if waiting for her execution.

Dr. Mullen, her creator, still works at the G.R.F. Clinic that Father used to own, but which is now in the process of being converted to a charitable foundation under the strict supervision of Emma's dad. They continue to do genetic research but no more human cloning. Instead their research now centres on curing diseases.

He's checked up on Ariel a few times, and me too, since the operation. I'm still so angry I can barely stand to have him near me, but what choice do I have? Let's face it, who understands your make-up better than the guy who made you?

He's over at the house within half an hour. He asks me to leave the room so he can examine Ariel. He comes out looking cheerful. He calls Mother and me over.

"Nothing wrong with her!" he assures us in his very posh British accent. He has a round face and watery blue eyes and hair the colour of wheat.

"How do you know?" I demand. I don't trust him.

"Because I've examined her and talked to her. She is simply trying to please. Your mother tells me you gave her a little talk the other day, Miranda."

"Yes," I agree. "A *little* one. And she's never paid any attention to my complaints before!"

"She's a thoughtful child, though, isn't

she," he said. "And she decided that she was not being a good sister. She's trying hard to be one now."

"Well, tell her to go back to the old one," I demand. "She's weird now."

"I can't make her do anything," he says. "I'm sure you wouldn't want me to. Let her find her own way. Be patient. She'll be who she's going to be. I think you'll find this is just part of her learning to be in the real world," he says to Mother.

I go into our room and find her sitting on her bed. When she sees me she gets a big bright smile that looks phony as anything and says, "Hello! Let's have some fun!"

"What did Dr. Mullen say to you?" I ask, suspicious of this put-on cheerfulness.

"He said that I must tell you that he is my doctor and all our talks are private."

So he's told her not to tell me anything, I think. Why?

"But you can talk to *me*," I coax. "I'm Miranda."

She looks confused, so I relent. I'd better not add to her confusion. It might make her worse. "Never mind," I say, "you just do what Dr. Mullen tells you."

She smiles. "I will be happy! Let's go have fun!"

"What do you want to do?"

"Have fun!"

I try to think. She's loved swimming ever since she came to live with us. Father, to his credit, spent a lot of time teaching her.

"A swim before dinner?" I suggest.

"Yes! A swim."

So we change into our suits, except I have to help her find hers as she seems to have forgotten where it might be, and we go out to the pool. I jump right in. It's cool and feels glorious. Ariel stands by the edge for a minute staring at me as I tread water.

"C'mon, jump!" I yell.

She jumps in after me, and proceeds to sink right to the bottom! When she surfaces she flails about and swallows water and is obviously in distress. I have to put my arms around her and pull her out.

"Are you crazy?" I pant once we are sitting by the side of the pool. "You have to swim!"

She looks terrified.

"Do I know how?"

I wipe the water out of my eyes and stare at her.

I don't care what Dr. Mullen says. Something is wrong.

Chapter 6

"Miranda, dinner," Mother calls.

I drag Ariel into the house and help her get changed. She's so much like she was when I first met her in that lab, I can't get over it.

We go to the dinner table. Mother and Father are sipping their wine. Lorna has put out our salad already.

"How are you, Ariel?" Father enquires.

"I am fine, thank you," she replies.

I sit down and stab a piece of lettuce.

"Well, she's not," I announce. "She's acting as if the last few weeks never happened. She almost drowned right now. She forgot how to swim!"

"I'm sure she didn't forget, Miranda," Mother says. "She simply didn't want to swim."

"That's why she sank to the bottom of the pool?" I say sarcastically.

Father smiles at Ariel. "Were you teasing?" he asks.

"Teasing?" She brightens. "I am having fun!" she says.

"There," says Father. "She was just pulling your leg. You need to relax, Miranda. Don't see a disaster around every corner."

"You can hardly blame me," I say bitterly.

"That's true," he says, trying not to look pained at my words. "But we concealed things for your own good. And now you know. There are no more hidden conspiracies. You need to stop reading so much into everything."

I suppose he's right. I'm suspicious of everything these days.

"Let's have fun!" Ariel says brightly.

"Yes, that's the spirit," Father agrees. "Now eat your dinner."

After dinner I do my homework and then decide to watch a tape. Ariel has been quietly reading on her bed.

"Want to watch *Mary Poppins*?" I say. I always watch that when I'm feeling blue or confused — actually, I'll watch it any time.

She nods, and looks pleased. We go into the family room. As soon as the movie starts she begins to mutter quietly under her breath. I realize that she is saying every line. She knows the entire movie by heart.

"I didn't know you liked this movie," I say.

"Oh, yes," she says. "We watch it every day. It's my favourite."

"Who's we?" I ask.

She looks worried suddenly. "Who's we? Who's we?"

"Yes," I say. "Who watches it with you?"

But she won't answer. She continues to mouth the words and is so happy that I feel it would be cruel to keep pestering her. I leave her watching and go to my room to phone Emma. "Hi!" I say.

"Hi! Is it cool? They never suspected?"

"What?"

"The acting class!"

"Oh that! I'd almost forgotten. No, nothing."

"What about Ariel?"

"We've had Dr. Mullen here and everything. He swears she's fine. Except right after he leaves she jumps in the pool and then seems to forget how to swim."

"That's a dangerous thing to forget."

"Mother and Father think she's just having me on, but I think something is seriously wrong. Father gave me this speech at dinner, which sounded good at the time, about how I can't keep being suspicious all the time . . . "

"Hey, you have a right to be!" Emma declares.

"That's what I think," I agree. "But I don't know what to do. Listen, can you ask your father if Dr. Mullen is behaving? Nothing strange or bad going on at the clinic? He's not working on mind control now or any bizarre thing we should know about?"

"Sure, I'll ask," Emma says. "But if there is anything going on that shouldn't be, Dr. Mullen wouldn't let my dad see it. Maybe *we* should go check it out."

"How? Just walk in?"

"No. Let me see if I can work on Dad. I'll think of something."

"Great. Thanks."

"Hey," Emma says. "What about Dale?"

"Is he gorgeous, or what?" I sigh.

"Or what!" she agrees. "But listen to this! Michael Lebowitz called to ask me if I want to go to a movie on Saturday."

"No!"

"Yes!"

"Why didn't you tell me right away?"

"I was saving it. I couldn't believe it. 'Course, Mom doesn't want me to go. 'You're too young to be going out alone.' Blah, blah, blah."

"Too bad Dale and I can't come with you," I giggle.

"Yeah, well, Michael's older brother is

going to drive us and take us home. I think Mom may come around. I'm still working on her."

Just then Ariel comes in. "Go away," I say, waving her out of the room. She scurries out.

Emma and I are still chattering away when Mother comes into the room dragging Ariel. "I found her walking down the driveway. What did you say to her?"

"Emma, hang on," I say, then turn to my mother. "I told her to go away. I'm talking to Emma."

"She obviously took you literally," Mother says. "Careful what you say."

I shake my head. "Did you hear that?" I say to Emma.

"Yeah."

"See what I mean?"

"Something's not right, I agree with you," Emma says. "I'll see what I can get out of my dad."

"Okay. Talk later."

Mother is turning to leave when suddenly Ariel clutches her head. She lets out a small squeal.

"What is it?" Mother asks.

I run over to Ariel and kneel down by her.

"My eyes," she says. "My eyes are behaving strangely. I do not see clearly."

I must go white as a sheet because I feel like all the blood has drained from my head and dropped to my feet. I am so lightheaded I can't stand. I sink to the floor.

"Miranda," Mother says alarmed. "Are you all right? Come. Lie down." She drags me over to my bed and puts some pillows under my knees. I'm sure I was about to faint.

I turn my head and see her walk Ariel over to her bed. She speaks in that really calm voice she gets when she's trying not to panic. "What is the matter with your eyes?"

That's how it started with me, of course. One minute I was fine and healthy and the next minute my eyesight had gone blurry and they discovered I had Von Hippel-Lindau disease and that my body was riddled with tumours. The ones in your spinal cord and brain, they make your vision go fuzzy.

But Dr. Mullen gave Ariel every single test in the book and they told me she was just about as perfect as you could get. She didn't have the disease, which meant that mine must have been a spontaneous mutation. Although, I *had* secretly wondered if Dr. Mullen was telling the whole truth.

On the other hand, maybe Ariel *was* just more perfect than me. Maybe he'd just done a better job on her. Made a few little changes. Improvements.

But now if she has it too . . . Mother is laughing. She is laughing hysterically.

"What's so funny?" I say, trying to sit up.

Mother holds out a small piece of lint on her finger tip.

"Ariel had something in her eye," she says, still laughing.

"Really?"

"Really."

"Can you see now, Ariel?" I ask.

"Yes. I can see very well."

I flop back on the bed. That would have been too much.

"Shall we have fun?" she says.

I shake my head. "Bedtime," I say. But I am still not convinced there isn't something *very* wrong with her.

Chapter 7

Ariel is sound asleep, although I thought I heard her crying.

I can't sleep. Too many thoughts racing around in my head. It's just hard to accept how much things have changed in such a short time. For instance, a few weeks ago I would have thought myself incapable of lying to my parents. I am still surprised that I did it yesterday and that it felt so easy. But I suppose I have a lot of resentment built up. Fine, I admit it, I'm mad. Really mad.

I thought they were so noble, so honest, so good. And yet they were willing to sacrifice Ariel, *murder* her, let's not sugar-coat it, to save my life. She gives up her liver — I live, she dies. I insisted that we share the liver and it's worked out. But I still don't think they feel anything for her, except thankful that she saved me. Well, maybe they are *beginning* to like her. But this personality change, for instance. If it was me, they'd be all over it. Dragging me to a psychiatrist, no doubt, within seconds. But because it's her they are just willing to take Dr. Mullen's word for everything.

And actually who's to say they aren't in it with Dr. Mullen like they were last time? Maybe they've all agreed to lie to me. But why? And what exactly could they be lying about?

And then something suddenly occurs to me. I sit bolt upright in bed and I can feel myself break out into a sweat. I know my imagination is probably running away with me, but I can't shake this idea. I grab the phone and sneak out of my room. Mother and Father are asleep and the house is dark.

I hurry through the kitchen, the dining room, the living room, until I reach the far end of the house, the family room. I sink into the couch and call Emma. She has her own line so I never have to worry about waking her family. Sometimes she doesn't appreciate me waking her. I sleep a lot less than she does and this won't be my first late-night call.

"Emma?"

"Miranda?" She's groggy.

"Sorry to wake you, but this can't wait."

"What?"

"I know this is paranoid," I say. "But the swimming thing. People don't just suddenly forget how to swim, do they? I mean, you could change your attitudes, maybe even your personality, although I find that hard to swallow, but you can't just forget how to swim. And I'm sure she wasn't teasing me like my parents are saying. She kind of went along with that, but she didn't really seem to believe it."

"Yes. Go on."

"Well, then you add up all the other stuff. How she's talking different all of a sudden, how she doesn't seem to have any idea who she is anymore. I simply can't believe it's all because I told her off about a stupid shirt. Come on." I pause.

"You don't think . . . " Emma whispers. Then she stops.

"Emma," I whisper back, "what if it isn't *her*?"

"Oh my gosh."

"I'm a clone. She's a clone. What if this Ariel isn't the *real* Ariel? What if she's been *substituted*?"

"But why?" Emma exclaims. "Isn't it more likely, if there's an evil plot, that they've done something to her mind? Or even worse," she adds, "her mind is malfunctioning and there's some sort of problem with the whole cloning process?"

Just what I, too, have been worried about. And a malfunction would be worse. For Ariel. To lose your personality all of a sudden. It's true that Dr. Mullen had lots of failures before he succeeded with us. Maybe he didn't really succeed with her at all. Maybe she is malfunctioning. Does that mean it could happen to me? Maybe I'll be next. Maybe I'll suddenly forget to be who *I* am. After all, I've gotten sick once already — that certainly wasn't planned by Dr. Mullen.

"What ever it is, I'd better find out," I say, "for her and for me. One thing I'm sure of, something isn't right. After Dr. Mullen was here it was almost like he'd given her instructions to lighten up and have fun like the old Ariel, but this one has no idea how to do it. She just keeps repeating 'Let's have fun. Let's have fun.' "

"I asked my dad about the lab," Emma says.

"And?"

"Nothing. He says it's under strict supervision and Dr. Mullen is behaving. But your dad owns lots of clinics, doesn't he, all across the country?"

"There's another clinic here in town," I say.

"You know, not the research one, the one where I go. My pediatrician works there."

"Maybe he has other secret ones," Emma suggests. "After all, you didn't know about Dr. Mullen's clinic and that was one of your dad's."

"But how do I find out?" I say. "He won't want me to know. And are my parents in on it or not? It's terrible not being able to trust your parents," I add.

"Yeah, it's not right," Emma agrees. "It should be the other way around."

I laugh.

"Miranda?"

It is Ariel, standing by the door. "Hey, she's here."

"Talk to her," says Emma. "See if you can't get some more out of her."

"Right. See you tomorrow. Sorry about waking you up."

"I'm used to it," she says. "Maybe I should be a doctor. You've got me in good training for never sleeping."

"Not my favourite profession right now," I say to her. "Stick to singing. Bye."

"Bye."

Ariel is still standing by the door.

"What is it?" I ask.

"You were gone when I awoke. I must be sure that you are safe."

I roll my eyes, even though she can't see me. "Come in."

"It is dark."

"You can see in the dark," I say. "I can."

"I cannot."

"Since when?"

"I do not know how to answer that."

"What happened yesterday?" I demand.

"What do you mean?"

"You're different. What happened?"

"I am just trying to be Ariel."

"Why are you *trying* to be Ariel? *Aren't* you Ariel?"

"Yes," she says, but she sounds uncertain. "I am Ariel."

"Do you feel any different than you did a few days ago?" I press her.

"No."

"Did Dr. Mullen do anything to you?"

"No."

"Did he tell you how to behave?"

She doesn't answer.

"He did, didn't he?" I think I'm onto something. "What? What did he tell you?"

"Many things."

"What?"

"I cannot say. He says all our conversations are private. Secrets, like you and I have. I can keep a secret!"

This is too frustrating. Obviously Dr. Mullen is involved in something. But what? What?

She says, "Am I not a good Ariel? Are you unhappy?"

"You're different," I answer. "And yes, that makes me unhappy because I don't understand it."

"But I should not make you unhappy."

Aha! This might be her Achilles heel. She may have promised Dr. Mullen something, but the old Ariel was brought up to serve me. Indoctrinated. Even if this is a different Ariel, she may have been brought up the same way. Maybe if I play up what she owes me she'll have to tell me the truth.

"It makes me unhappy," I say, "not to know why you suddenly seem so different."

Long pause.

"I do not know what to do," she answers. "Dr. Mullen made me promise, but you are Miranda . . . "

"Come on," I say. "Let's go to the kitchen and get a snack. Remember how you love to eat chocolate sundaes late at night? Remember how that makes you feel better?"

I get up and take her hand. We walk through to the kitchen where I turn on the light.

"Why are you different?" I say. "You must tell me. You must."

She is staring at me wide-eyed, obviously distressed. As I stare back at her it strikes me again how identical we are — same long blond hair, blue eyes, high forehead, high cheekbones — but wait. I look closer.

"What's that?" I ask.

"What?"

"You have something over your eye."

She puts her hand up and covers the spot.

"It is, it is, a freckle," she says.

"You have a freckle?"

"I am not perfect. I am useless. I am not good for anything."

Suddenly she cries out and puts both hands to her head. "My head. It hurts. It hurts terribly."

"Go lie down in bed," I tell her. "I'll get Mother."

I rush to my parents' room and knock on the door. My stomach is all knotted up. Now what? Ariel really sounded like she was in pain.

"Mother? Father?"

"Come in."

Mother sits up in bed. "What is it?"

"It's Ariel. She has a terrible headache. I'm worried."

"I'm sure it's nothing, Miranda," Mother says. "She's been checked. She's fine. Give her a Tylenol and both of you get some sleep."

"But . . . "

"Miranda. It's the middle of the night. Not now. Go to bed. We'll check her in the morning. You are overreacting to everything. Headaches are normal. Everybody gets them."

"But . . . "

"Now!"

I turn and leave the room. Just another example of how little they care. If it had been me they would have been hysterical. Well, *I* care about her. And I won't let her down.

Chapter 8

I lie in bed, groggy, just waking up. I gave Ariel a Tylenol and then sat up with her as she whimpered in pain for what felt like hours. She fell asleep, clutching onto my hand. I had to extricate my hand from hers without waking her and finally was able to crawl into my own bed where I lay, staring into the darkness until it began to get light and I must have dropped off.

How do I find out if Ariel isn't Ariel? That freckle. I've never seen it on her, although I know they can appear suddenly if you've been in the sun. And we're always in the sun. But if she isn't Ariel, where is the real one? It is just starting to sink in what that could mean. Has she been kidnapped? If so, by whom? She was almost murdered once. Is her life in danger? Is she somewhere alone and terrified?

I notice that Ariel, or the child who says she is Ariel, is up already, standing by the window. She is quite still, gazing out. I have an idea. A simple one. "Ariel," I say.

No answer. No response. The real Ariel would have at least turned. This one doesn't even recognize her name.

"Ariel," I say again.

"Oh!" This time she turns. "Yes?"

"How are you?" I ask.

"My headache is better, but not gone."

"I'm going to try to get Mother to take you to the doctor," I say. "And if she won't, I will."

"You will?"

"Yes."

"Why?"

"Because I'm your big sister. I need to take care of you."

"No," she corrects me, "I am made for you."

"I thought we'd gotten past that," I chide her.

"Past that?"

"Over it. Over and done with. You aren't made for anyone but yourself."

"My self. What is that?"

Good question, I think. One I've thought a lot about since I found out I was a clone.

"Well, that's hard to say." By now I am almost positive I am not talking to Ariel. "It's who you are. Inside."

"I am made only for you."

I am totally positive Ariel had gotten over this stage. But if this one is telling the truth and is spouting all this garbage she must be another of Dr. Mullen's Miranda clones. And he swore there were no more.

"Look," I say intensely, "part of finding out who you are is by the choices you make. You have to think for yourself. You don't just do what everyone tells you."

"I do what *you* tell me," she says confidently. "And you do what your parents tell you."

"I used to do everything they told me," I agree, "until I discovered they'd been lying to me. And it's all right to do what other people tell you if you think about it and agree with it. But not if you are just doing it because you've been trained to."

She shakes her head, confused.

"You have to tell me who you really are," I say. "And where the real Ariel is."

She looks alarmed.

"Why?"

Now's the time to get tough. "You must. You need to listen to me, and I want to know."

"You just told me I do not have to listen."

Me and my big mouth. I'm trying to figure out how to get around this one when Lorna bustles in.

"Hurry up, you two. You'll be late. Miranda,

what do you want to wear? It's going to be a scorcher today."

"Shorts," I say. "And a short-sleeved shirt. And a sweater for school." Even when I wear shorts they are cuffed and ironed. Ariel prefers much less formal clothes.

"Ariel?"

She doesn't answer.

"Ariel? What do you want to wear?"

"I like the bright purple," she answers. That, at least, is like the old Ariel.

I take a quick shower, dress, then go find Mother. She's in the kitchen drinking coffee. I have to talk to her but I don't even know if I can trust her. And how do I bring up the whole "we might have an extra clone" thing? I decide to start simple.

"Mother," I say, "you must take Ariel to the doctor. She's sick."

"Ariel has just been seen by a very capable doctor," Mother says. "Please stop this, Miranda. You are obsessing."

Obsessing, am I? I'll give her obsessing.

"Yeah, well," I blurt out, "I think it's much worse than her just being sick." I take a breath. "I think she might not even be Ariel."

"Meaning?" Mother says.

"Meaning I think she might be another clone. And I'm very worried about where the real Ariel is and what's happened to her."

Mother rolls her eyes.

"Stop that!" I say. "You have to listen to me. I'm not being paranoid."

"You are," she says. "You are worried the whole thing is happening over again, except to Ariel this time. I promise you that everything is fine. Why would we need a second clone? It's ridiculous. I think that maybe you need to talk to someone."

"Like a shrink?"

"Yes."

"And I tell this shrink I'm a clone and he puts me away in the loony bin."

"I guess that's a problem," she admits.

"No kidding. Anyway, I don't need a shrink. I need you to listen to me."

"Obviously, if Ariel really gets sick, we'll have Dr. Mullen look at her again. But not until then. He was just here and he says she is fine."

"Not Dr. Mullen! He can't be trusted. And he's not a pediatrician, anyway."

"But he knows you both, and your case," she counters.

Ariel comes in. She sits primly at the table and eats one piece of toast. Her fresh-squeezed lemon juice sits by her plate. I push it over to her.

"Take a big drink," I say. "It's your favourite."

She takes a gulp — "Aaargh!" and spits it out. "That is horrible!"

"But only yesterday you loved it," I say, looking meaningfully at Mother.

But Mother refuses to acknowledge that there is anything wrong. She ignores the entire thing, except to reprimand Ariel for her manners. As if that's important right now. "Come along, girls. Time to go."

When we get to school Ariel goes off and I find Emma.

"So?" she says.

"I'm sure it isn't her. She practically admitted it. She doesn't really answer to her name, she hates lemon juice . . . "

"What can we do?" Emma asks as we hurry to class.

"We have to get into the clinic," I say. "Dr. Mullen must be up to something. But what? It has to be him, don't you think?"

"If there's something bad going on we can assume that he's behind it, yeah," Emma agrees. "The question is what we can do about it."

Classes drag by. I spend my time trying to think up a new name for the one who isn't Ariel. If she'll let me do it, I'll be absolutely positive. Ariel loved her name. I should call her Poser. But that wouldn't be nice, would it? If she is posing, she's doing it because Dr. Mullen is making her. Maybe she should be called Dupe.

What about something simple, like the name of a flower? A name of her own would help her think of herself as an individual, who can think for herself. If I could get her to do that, maybe I could find out what happened to the real Ariel. I think hard. I know! Not a flower. Adam. The first man. Eve. First woman. She should be Eve. For being brand new.

I hurry to find her at lunch.

"Do you know the story of Genesis?" I ask her.

She shakes her head.

"Well," I say as we sit down, "there is this book called the Bible. And it tells stories. Stories of how the world began."

"Oh!" she says. "I do know. Myths of creation. I have studied them. Genesis is Adam and Eve, correct?"

"Yes," I say. "And since you are starting a new life, I think you should have a new name. Eve."

She looks at me bewildered. "You do not want me to be Ariel?"

"No," I say firmly, "because even though you won't admit it to me, I know you aren't Ariel. So it's wrong to use her name."

She begins to object, but I continue. "And you should have your own name, shouldn't you? I gave Ariel her name. And now I'll give you your name. Eve. And you'll be my other new little sister."

She looks at me then, and her eyes are full of hope. "You will still like me? You won't want to dispose of me if I am not Ariel?"

That's it! That's what Dr. Mullen threatened her with. I take her hand. "Of course not! You'll be Eve. You'll be my sister, too. But you have to help me find Ariel."

She clutches the table. "Miranda!"

Just then Emma and Susan join us.

"What is it?" I say, alarmed.

"My head. It hurts."

I flip my phone open and call Mother.

"Yes, dear?"

"Mother, Ariel's got another horrible headache. If you don't come and take her to the doctor now, I'll do it myself. And not Dr. Mullen. My doctor."

"Miranda!"

"I'll tell the principal you aren't available and I'll get a cab over there with her."

"I'll be right there," she says grimly.

"Good." I hang up. "Come on, Eve," I say, "let's go wait at the front. Emma, can you tell the office we're going?"

When Mother comes we get into the car and I buckle Eve up. And then I say, "Mother, meet Eve."

"What do you mean?"

"I mean this is not Ariel. This is Eve."

"Miranda," she says, "that is quite enough. I will take Ariel to the doctor, but stop all this nonsense."

I don't reply. I try to think how I'm going to find the real Ariel. Where could she be? And why was this switch made?

Chapter 9

I am terrified by what the doctor might find. Is this a repeat of my disease? And if so, why? How? Mine was a spontaneous mutation, I thought, not something in my DNA. I am sitting in the front seat and the radio is on so I figure Eve can't really hear too much. In a low voice, I say, "Mother, I want you to tell me the truth. Did Dr. Mullen ever figure out why I got my disease?"

She pauses for minute before she answers. I think she is trying to decide whether or not to be honest.

"Mother!"

"It was a genetic mutation," she answers. "Spontaneous. He checked Ariel thoroughly and she does not have it. In fact, her genetic structure seems to be quite perfect. At any rate, her symptoms are different. She has a headache, not blurry vision."

"But Ariel doesn't have it," I point out to

her. "This is Eve. She's sick. We don't know where Ariel is."

Mother doesn't answer, but I can see her gritting her teeth.

"Of course," I say, thinking out loud, "If it was a spontaneous thing with me, then why would Eve have it? That makes no sense."

"No, it doesn't," Mother says. "So let's just get this over with."

"Dr. Corne hasn't ever seen Eve, has he?" I ask.

"Stop calling her that!"

"Has he?" I persist.

"No, he has not seen Ariel. You know that."

"Good. At least I'll know he isn't in on it."

I turn to the back seat. "Eve. How are you?"

"My head hurts," she complains.

We drive into the parking lot and I help Eve out. It is so hot it's hard to walk, even from the car to the front door of the clinic. Eve stumbles. I practically carry her inside. The air conditioning feels wonderful.

There is the usual waiting room filled with screaming babies and fighting children. Mother makes sure we are taken through right away. The perks of owning the place! I insist on going in with Eve and Mother. I don't trust Mother to go in alone. Who knows, maybe Dr. Corne is in on all this too —

although I really doubt it. When I was sick he diagnosed me and then Dr. Mullen took over.

"Hello, Miranda," he says in his usual serious way. "I'm so pleased to hear about your full recovery. And Ariel here turned up just at the right time for you, didn't she?" He turns to Eve and extends his hand. "Hello. I'm Dr. Corne."

She doesn't respond.

Dr. Corne calls for his nurse and then sends both me and Mother out of the room. We sit and wait in the examining room. He comes out after what seems like ages.

"I'd like your permission to do an MRI of her brain, and perhaps an angiogram," he says. "I have some concerns."

Mother consents. She calls Father. Eventually he shows up. We wait. Finally Dr. Corne calls us in to his office. He motions for us to sit down.

"Ariel is resting in one of the examining rooms," he says. "I'm afraid you need to be prepared for some very bad news." I hold my breath. "She has a brain tumour."

"You mean tumours, like I did?" I ask.

"No, Miranda. One brain tumour. Almost certainly cancer already in an advanced stage. I doubt we'll be able to operate. Have you noticed any other symptoms besides the headaches? Clumsiness? Nausea? Even a personality change?"

"Yes," we all say at once.

"Definitely a personality change," I say.

"That is a common symptom, and often the most distressing one, as it feels like you've lost a person close to you." He turns to Father. "You were able to help Miranda in your research clinic. I understand you've given it over to a charitable foundation. But maybe they could still help. There are trials going on for this type of cancer, but they are hard to get into. If you can pull some strings, use your contacts . . . "

I can't believe it. I am so stunned I can hardly breathe. So it really *is* Ariel and she's got a brain tumour, just like Jessica — Mother and Father's first child. Jessica died from hers and it sounds like Ariel will too.

"But how did she get it?"

"Hard to say," he answers. "If she worked in a factory I'd say it could be exposure to chemicals. We're finding that is a common cause. Do you know if she had any chemical exposure before she came to you?"

"No, I'm not sure," Mother lies.

But she grew in a chemical soup, I think. And then I remember the articles about the defective mouse clones — the ones that seemed normal at first, but then started to exhibit bizarre physical symptoms as they got older. And I start to wonder about my own illness, too. But there is no time for that now.

They keep talking about treatment and what to do, but I don't really hear it. I can't take all this in! I was so convinced that this wasn't Ariel. And now it seems that it is, but that she's going to die!

I get up, run from the room, and go to find Ariel. The nurse shows me into her examining room. She is getting dressed and I notice her scar. I'm so stupid! Why didn't I just think to check to see if she had a scar. Only Ariel would have one — so she couldn't be a different clone. I've been sunk in paranoia and I've been no help to Ariel at all. She's ill and all I've done is make it worse. I go over and hug her. "We'll find a cure," I say. "We will." She says nothing. I help her get dressed and then Mother and Father come to fetch us.

I sit in the back seat of the car with Ariel as Mother drives, and hold her hand.

"Mother," I say, "you were right. While Ariel was dressing I saw her scar — only Ariel could have that scar."

"I should have thought of that myself," Mother says.

"I am very sick," Ariel interrupts.

"Yes," I agree.

"I have to go to a hospital," she says.

"You do," Mother says from the front, "but we don't know which one yet, dear. Father has to call Dr. Mullen."

"Dr. Mullen said she was fine!" I object.

"Still," Mother says, "he knows all the latest experimental treatments, where they are happening. He's our best bet."

"Dr. Mullen knows everything," Ariel says.

I hate this. She's just like she was before. She's lost everything that made her herself.

We get home and put Ariel to bed. I go to the kitchen and listen to the messages to see if anyone has called. Mother and Father use the other line in the living room to call Dr. Mullen.

The first message is something for Mother, about a charity dinner. I save it. The second one is for me, from Emma.

"Hey. I'm home. Call me."

The third one is another for Mother. So's the fourth. The fifth one is Ariel.

"*Miranda*? *Help me. Help me.*" And then a click and the phone going dead.

I play it over.

"*Miranda, help me. Help me.*"

She sounds desperate. Frightened. I stand

frozen, staring at the phone. I have just accepted that Ariel is here. But then how could she be calling me and asking for help, when I was with her most of the day? I check the time on the message. 10:05 AM. We were in school then. I am hopelessly confused.

I save the message and run to our room. Ariel, or Eve, or whoever the heck she is, is lying in bed. "Ariel," I say, "did you call me today?"

"I called your name."

"No, I mean did you phone me?"

"Phone? No," she says. "I was with you all day. Why would I telephone you?"

"Are you positive?"

"Yes. I was not aware I could phone you. And why would I? You were at school with me. Should I want to talk to you, would I not come and find you, instead of phoning you?"

She hasn't lost her ability to reason.

I run back to the phone and go through all the numbers on the caller display. I find number five. *Unknown number*.

I let out a scream of frustration, then call Emma.

"Emma!"

"Hi!"

"Can you come over? No wait. Better if I come there. I'll see if Mother'll drive me."

"Sure," Emma says. "What's up?"

"Tell you later," I say as Mother walks into the kitchen. And then I remember that I haven't erased the message. So I play it for her.

"Miranda, Ariel has a brain tumour! She's forgotten already that she called you. You weren't with her every minute of today, were you?"

"No," I admit. "But she says she never would have even thought of calling me."

"Stop this nonsense, Miranda," she says. Then she looks at me sympathetically, for a moment letting down the guard she seems to have put up. "We have a very sick child and you have to adjust to the fact that she may not get better. But Father and I will always be here for you. You know that, don't you?" In a flash I understand why she's been so cold. She's terrified. She's afraid she's lost me forever. She's afraid I'll never be able to love her again. The scary thing is — she might be right.

"But you're going to try to help her, aren't you?" I ask.

"Of course we are. Dr. Mullen is on his way over now."

"Can you drive me to Emma's first?"

She thinks for a minute. "Perhaps that

would be a good idea. Dr. Mullen can examine Ariel and I'll pick you up around nine. What about dinner?"

"I'll grab a sandwich there," I say.

So off we go to Emma's. Living outside the city on a big spread is annoying. I can't go anywhere without being driven. Probably part of their plan, I think. Easier to control me that way. But something is out of control here, and I have to find out what it is, fast.

The scar proves it's Ariel. But the phone call says it isn't.

Chapter 10

Emma lives in a bungalow at the bottom of a short street. The street ends in a cul-de-sac and there is a hiking path that begins there, affectionately known by the locals as Doggy Poop Trail — for obvious reasons. Emma has a dog, a golden retriever, and I arrive just as she's getting ready to take him outside. It's almost six o'clock and it's still broiling hot. We decide to take Merv for a short walk up the trail.

"Miranda," Emma's mom calls out, "we haven't eaten yet. Will you eat with us?"

"Sure," I say, "thanks."

Emma and I set off. The trail winds up the hills behind the street and we quickly get a lovely view of the city. The trail is packed with other hikers, most of them with dogs. Fortunately Merv is pretty well trained and doesn't lunge at the other dogs, which is a good thing since half of them seem to be pit-bulls. Guess I'm not the only paranoid person around — the only reason anyone could want such an ugly dog is for protection.

Emma and I discuss all the latest news. It's hard to know whether Ariel is sick or if it isn't Ariel at all. The thing is, if it isn't Ariel, the real Ariel is out there somewhere and I need to help her. But how do I find out? We seem to have reached a dead end.

"I wish we could drive," I sigh.

"Why?"

"Dr. Mullen is on his way over to our house right now. If we could drive to his clinic and get in while he's away, maybe we could find out what's going on."

Emma looks at me in amazement. "Talk about personality change."

"Meaning?"

"Meaning you know very well that two months ago you never would have thought of that."

"It's true. Do you think Ariel has a tumour?" I ask. "I suppose that could explain everything, and she really is Ariel after all."

"It does explain everything," Emma says. "And the scar is pretty definite evidence. But I'm with you. I still feel like something isn't right. And why did she get sick? I thought Dr. Mullen said she was perfect." As we turn to start down the trail she says, "Maybe one of my brothers would drive us over there."

"You think?"

"We can ask. Say you're supposed to pick up a special prescription or something. They won't know the difference."

It never ceases to amaze me how quickly Emma can come up with a good cover story.

On the way down we pass all kinds of people who are jogging up the trail. I find walking in this heat quite enough. I hope I never turn into that kind of a crazy adult.

Emma has two older brothers: Josh, who is eighteen, and Ben, who is sixteen. They are both home for dinner because Emma's mom insists everyone be there for Friday night Sabbath dinners. She lights the candles, then says the blessings over wine and bread. I know all the Sabbath blessings by heart, I've been over for dinner so many times.

We have a great meal of roasted chicken and I find I am starving. I've hardly eaten the last few days, I've been so worried.

Emma works on Josh after dinner until he agrees to drive us and wait while we go into the clinic. We figure it's safer that way — we won't just disappear like maybe Ariel did. The clinic is only about a ten-minute drive from Emma's house, and soon Josh is pulling up in front.

"Hurry up," he warns me. "I have a date tonight."

"I will," I say. "Emma, want to come?"

Emma says, "Sure," and we hurry to the door and ring the bell.

Ms Yellow Teeth, otherwise known as Jean the nurse, answers. "Miranda. What can I do for you?"

"Dr. Mullen called me at Emma's," I lie, "and said we should meet him here. He said to wait in the office."

She opens the door for us. "Come in."

We follow her into the foyer.

"Best wait here," she says. "He's been out for a while, I'm sure he won't be long."

We sit down.

As soon as she goes off to do whatever it is she does — I briefly wonder why a nurse would be working at a clinic that no longer has any patients — I motion to Emma. We get up and I lead the way to Dr. Mullen's office. I try the door handle. Not locked! We step in.

Dr. Mullen is seated at his desk, smiling.

Emma and I jump a mile.

His grin broadens.

"I've been expecting you."

I can't answer. Emma grimaces.

"Have a seat, girls."

"My brother is waiting outside," Emma warns. Neither of us moves from the door.

"Yes, well then, I'll be brief," Dr. Mullen says. "I understand, Miranda, that you are trying to convince your parents that Ten is not really Ten."

"I think it's a possibility," I say, my heart still beating so hard I can barely hear my own voice. "And her name is Ariel now."

"I want you to stop talking to your parents this way."

"Why?" I ask.

"Because they might eventually believe you. And that could cause a lot of trouble for me."

I don't like the sound of this. Emma and I are standing close to each other as if that will protect us. From what, though?

"Just spit it out," Emma demands.

He smiles again. "Yes, good plan. The direct approach. Here's the thing. Ten has been removed. That child is not Ten. She is a defective clone I made immediately before I made Number Ten. I call her Eleven at the moment because she is actually older than Ten, and I name them each year by their age. Tests on her revealed that she was imperfect but I decided to keep her as a back-up should I ever need her, and now I find I do."

I grab Emma's hand.

"But where's Ariel?" I exclaim.

"Ariel is somewhere safe," he says.

"But why? Why have you done it?"

"You don't need the details of why or where. All you need to know is that if you tell your parents, I will kill Ariel. You know I am capable," he says lightly, "of doing so. I can always harvest her DNA before I do away with her. So you and Emma should just forget this little talk and try to help the other child. She'll need it."

"How do we know Ariel is safe?" Emma demands.

"You don't," he says. "But I am telling you that she is, and that she will remain so. Unless you force me to kill her to cover up her abduction." He stands up. "Are we clear?"

"You can't!" I say.

"I believe I can," he says.

"Wait," I say. "What about her scar? It *must* be Ariel."

"I made an incision in Number Eleven and stitched her up again in order to convince your parents that she is the same girl. They cannot discover that I am still doing human experiments. And now you must go."

He ushers us out of his office, down the corridor and out the front door. We stand there so shocked we can't move. Josh honks. That startles us. We clamber back into the car.

"You girls look like you've seen a ghost," Josh says. "Everything okay?"

"Can I sleep over?" I ask Emma in a small voice.

"You'd better," she says.

"What's up?" Josh asks again.

"Nothing!" We both answer at once.

Josh drives us back to Emma's house. I call my parents. My dad answers.

"What did Dr. Mullen say?" I ask.

"He was very sorry to hear about the test results. And he says he doesn't know of any treatments. He says we have to prepare for the worst."

"There must be something," I say.

"I don't think so, Miranda. Are you ready to come home?"

"No. I'm sleeping over here tonight."

"I think Ariel needs you," he says.

"I know. But I need to be here."

"All right," Father says. "We'll come get you tomorrow. Call."

I hang up. Emma and I go to her room and sit on the bed. I stare at her.

"What are we going to do?" I say.

"Something," she says, voice determined. "We are *not* going to let him get away with it."

"But what?" I repeat. "And poor Eve. To him she's just some experiment gone wrong. I mean, to go so far as to cut her open just to give her a scar. He's horrible!"

"He is," Emma agrees. "And we have to stop him."

"Why would he tell us all that?" I wonder aloud. "The scar just about had us convinced. He didn't have to tell us, did he?"

"Yeah," Emma agrees. "Maybe none of it's true! Maybe he's trying to confuse us."

"But he'd figure that we would consider that," I counter. "So maybe he told us the truth, figuring we'd never believe him."

"Reverse psychology," Emma muses.

"We'll have to follow him," I say. "If it's true, he'll lead us to Ariel. We just have to figure out how to do it."

Chapter 11

Saturday morning, and we have it all worked out. Ben agrees to rent his bicycle to me for the weekend. Emma tried to get him to just lend it to us but that was out of the question. "Brothers!" Emma mutters.

It's nine AM when we set off. It takes us about half an hour to get to the clinic. We both have baseball caps under our helmets, which we pull down so that they act as disguises as well as protection from the sun. We also borrowed baseball jerseys from Ben so we look like two kids on our way to a game. Since it's already blistering hot out, we arrive out of breath and sweating.

The clinic is set back from the street with its own driveway. There's only one way out, so Emma and I plant ourselves behind a large truck parked just at the end of the driveway. We spot Dr. Mullen around ten-fifteen as he drives past us into the clinic driveway.

Both Emma and I figure that Ariel isn't at the clinic. It's being closely watched now and has a different administrator in charge. Dr. Mullen must have Ariel stashed somewhere else. But where?

Around eleven he goes out. It isn't easy to follow him on the bikes but we just manage to keep his van in view. And he doesn't go far. He stops at a small strip mall and hurries into a Starbucks. We peer in the window and see that he is sitting with a man and they are deep in conversation. The man then hands a briefcase over to Mullen, who takes it and leaves. We sneak around the corner in the nick of time so he doesn't catch sight of us.

He doesn't go back to the clinic, though. He gets onto Palm Canyon Drive and heads south.

Now it's impossible to keep up on our bikes, but thanks to bad traffic and lights, we manage to keep him in view for a while. Eventually we lose him altogether, and we pull up at a big intersection to decide what to do.

"Look, look," Emma says. She points left. Down the street is a large industrial park and what appears to be Dr. Mullen's van parked outside the building closest to us.

There are rows and rows of office buildings, all painted a pale pink, with mauve slate roofs. Set behind those are a group of larger buildings that look like warehouses of one sort or another. We turn down the street and move closer. The van looks the same as his but we can't be sure. Why didn't I think to memorize his plate number? And I'm supposed to be so smart.

"What do you think?" I pant.

"No one would suspect," Emma says, "if that's where he's hiding her. But why here?"

"He's devious," I say. "No one would think to look here."

"The question is, how do we get in without being seen? How do we find out?"

"We wait until he leaves," she says. "And then we check it out.'

That seems the only logical answer so that's what we do. Since we don't have to watch the place we decide to go get lunch. We are overheated and need to cool off. We find a nice little place nearby that makes huge sandwiches. We both call home and say we're fine, but that we won't be back until dinner. By the time we return, Dr. Mullen's van is gone. We drive our bikes around the side of the building and leave them there. Then we try the front door. It's locked. We walk around to the back where there's another door but it, too, is locked.

We are just about to give up and are heading around to the front when the front door opens. We flatten ourselves against the side wall. A large man walks out. He lights a cigarette and walks down the path.

I know we have to act fast. I motion to Emma. We sprint to the front door and into the building. There is a long corridor ahead of us. We have to get out of it or he'll see us as soon as he returns. There are doors off the corridor. I open the first one. An office. Empty of people. Full of computers. The next door is the same.

"Hurry," Emma hisses. We open the third door. A man in a white lab coat is standing beside all sorts of equipment, test tubes, vats, computers. He whirls around and sees us. We back out. Right into the cigarette man who grabs us each by our jerseys and lifts us into the air.

"You two lost?" he growls.

"Yes," Emma says.

"Well, get out of here," he snarls, "and don't come back!" He starts to drag us down the corridor. But the other man calls, "Hold up a minute. Don't let them go!"

He runs out and takes a good look at me.

He comes closer and knocks the hat off my head. "Look who it is," he says.

"Hey, she looks just like the other one!" the cigarette man says.

"You must be Miranda," the other man smiles. He is a short, skinny fellow, completely bald, but young, maybe twenty-five at the most.

"Get off me," I yell. I try to fight, but I'm being held in the air and all I can do is flail around.

"Bring them," the short guy says.

Emma and I both protest and shout, but who's going to hear us? The short guy points to a door. The big guy throws us in the room. And we hear the door lock.

We both run at the door and bang on it and turn the knob, all the stupid things you see people do in bad movies but we do it anyway. It's useless, of course.

I look around. No windows. A few long tables with lab equipment and a few chairs.

"This isn't good," I say to Emma.

"That's for sure," she agrees. "If he was willing to kill Ariel, who's to say he won't just kill us too?"

"And no one has . . . wait a minute," I say. "I've got my cell." I laugh.

"And I've got mine!" Emma exclaims.

Emma pulls hers out but she gets no service.

I try mine. It works! Eve answers.

"Eve!" I exclaim. "It's me! Miranda."

"Hello Miranda."

"I need help. I'm in trouble. I'm stuck in Dr. Mullen's lab, in the industrial park off . . . "

"Trouble?" she interrupts.

"Yes!"

"Dr. Mullen is here with me. He would like to know what trouble."

"No! Don't tell him! He's the trouble. You have to . . . "

Suddenly I hear his voice.

"Hello?"

"Put Eve back on," I say. "Or my parents."

"Your parents are speaking to a specialist I brought over. I am examining Number Eleven. It occurs to me there is more to discover about her condition." His lab rat, I think. "Oh, just a moment, my phone is ringing."

He hands the phone back to Eve.

"Eve," I say, "we're trapped. You have to help me . . . "

Then Dr. Mullen's voice again.

"I thought I warned you to leave all this alone, Miranda. I just got a call from my colleagues. Apparently you are my guest."

"Yes," I exclaim. "And you'd better let us go!"

Just then the door opens and the big lug comes back in. He grabs my phone and Emma's, walks out and slams the door.

"Great?" I exclaim. "Just great!"

"What?" says Emma.

"It's Dr. Mullen. I got through to Eve but Dr. Mullen was there and now we're really in trouble."

We stare at each other.

"I'm sorry, Emma," I say. "I never should have let you get involved. I just didn't think. I didn't realize how dangerous it could get."

Emma throws her arms around me and gives me a hug.

"It's okay," she says. "We had to try to save Ariel. I guess we should have gone to my dad, though. We're playing in the big leagues here. Way over our heads."

I sink down on one of the chairs. She's right. Or is she?

"Maybe," I say. "But I should be smarter than all of them. Dr. Mullen made me that way, after all. I just have to think. I just have to think."

Chapter 12

I look around. They've stuck us in some kind of lab. Emma and I check out what's around us. There are little bottles and vials and test tubes all over the long table, but I have no idea what most of them are. We do find some hydrochloric acid, which I know hurts like anything if you get it on you.

"When the big guy comes in next," Emma says, "we throw this at him and run."

"It'll burn him," I object.

"Oh, but it's all right for them to murder us. We should just sit here and take it, I suppose?"

Here again Emma and I have this difference between us. I want to be good. Emma doesn't care. But I realize that my wanting to be good could get us killed. And I have to think about Emma, not just me. I got her into this, after all.

"You're right," I say. "But I hate to do it."

"This is like war," Emma says. "We have to save ourselves."

"But this isn't a war and anyway, we aren't positive that they want to hurt us. Dr. Mullen believes that the end justifies the means. But does it ever?"

"Yes," says Emma. "Sometimes it does!"

"You shouldn't do to others what you wouldn't want done to yourself," I say.

"Do you think Mullen would let that stop him?" she counters.

She has a point. So we position ourselves on either side of the door, each one holding an open bottle of acid, and wait. And wait. And wait. I look at my watch. Three o'clock.

"Dr. Mullen's obviously making other clones," I say. "Did you see all that equipment? Why is he doing it? What's he up to? It's horrible to see first-hand how I was created."

"And yet," Emma smiles, "you still aren't perfect."

She can make me laugh even when we're trapped in a mad scientist's lab waiting to be killed.

"Yeah, how's that possible?" I say.

"It's not just possible," says Emma, "it's necessary. Now if you were perfect — the thing you are always striving for, by the way — you wouldn't be human."

"What's the matter with Dr. Mullen?" I

ask. "Can't he see what he's doing is wrong?"

"He thinks he knows what's best for everyone," Emma says.

"Yeah," I agree, "dictators think that too. Never mind dictators, look at my parents. They were willing to kill Ariel to save me."

"Dad always tells me that I have to do what is right," Emma says, "and not worry about the consequences."

"I told Eve that her choices make her who she is. But, Emma, I can't get away from this — people make choices for the weirdest reasons. Half my choices are made because I've been bred to be good. And the other half because I've been brought up to be good. So I'm *conditioned* to choose a certain way. I mean, how free am I?"

"Maybe we're all programmed like robots or, machines, you mean," Emma says. "If not by our genes then by our parents . . . "

"And friends," I interrupt, "and magazines and movies and . . . "

Our discussion is interrupted by the lock turning and the door opening. Don't do to others what you wouldn't want done to yourself. Still, we have to make sure he won't hurt us either. Well, I wouldn't want that stuff thrown in my face, so I aim for his hands. Emma hits him on the back of the neck. He yells, dances around, and drops the key. I grab it and Emma and I are out the door before he can grab us. Not that I think he could with his hands hurting like that.

We slam the door and lock him in. Then we look around.

"We have to find Ariel," I whisper. "And get out of here."

We are more careful this time. Instead of opening each door wide, we open each one a crack and sneak a peek in.

The first door opens on a room with a woman sitting at a computer. She doesn't notice me. The next door leads to a room full of equipment. Behind the third door is a large partition. I can't tell what's on the other side without going in. We slip in and shut the door behind us.

I peek around the partition. The room is separated with large screens into three sections. Sitting directly in front of me on a cot is Ariel!

"Ariel!"

"Miranda!"

She leaps off the cot and throws herself into my arms.

"You found me! You're so smart! You are so good! How did you do it! Hi, Emma." She hugs Emma too. "Are we leaving? Can we go home?"

"Yes," I say. "Let's get out of here before Dr. Mullen gets back."

"Dr. Mullen is here," Ariel says. "He was just in to visit me."

"Oh, no," I groan. "Then he'll find the big lug any second."

"The back door," Emma suggests. "There's a back exit, remember?"

"Yes," I say. "Let's make a run for it."

I take Ariel's hand and we creep toward the door. I hear it open. It's probably Dr. Mullen. I point at the partition. Emma nods. We both push it and it crashes over. I recognize Dr. Mullen's voice as he yells. The only trouble is that the partition is now against the door and although he's under it, we can't get out.

"Get this off me," he shouts.

"Not unless you let us go," I shout back.

"Can't do that. Help!" he starts to call at the top of his lungs.

I whisper to Emma. "I'm the strongest. You and Ariel lift it up. I'll shove him out of our way. Then we run!"

She nods and motions for Ariel to help her lift the partition. They do, and it falls backwards. Dr. Mullen is trying to get up but I don't give him a chance. I push him down and we all shoot past him out into the hallway.

There are a couple of people in the hall, but they are coming out of the offices toward the front of the building. The corridor toward the back door is clear, although there are one or two heads peeking out of offices.

"Run!" I hiss.

We run. A young woman rushes out of a door and tries to stop us. I fight her off, giving her a good kick in the knees. Her legs buckle. We reach the end of the corridor and the door.

The door is locked. But it isn't a deadbolt that we can open from the inside. It must be locked from the outside. We're trapped. Quickly I look around. There are corridors going off from the back door on either side. One is clear of people.

"Come on," I say. I push them both to the right. "Check all the doors."

"This room is filled with stuff," Ariel calls to us. It is filled with boxes almost up to the ceiling.

"At least we can hide in here," I say. We dash in, shut the door behind us, and crouch at the back behind the boxes.

"Are you all right?" I say to Ariel, trying to catch my breath.

"He hasn't hurt me."

"What happened?" I ask.

Emma interrupts. "You can talk about all this later," she says, "but right now shouldn't we be thinking about getting out of here? In case you've forgotten," she says to me, "Dr. Mullen *did* threaten something very nasty if we got involved. And he's sure to be checking all the offices as we speak."

She's right. We have to get out. But how on earth? We're locked in a building full of his people. There are no windows. No phones. And no one has any idea where we are.

"But there must be a way," I mutter aloud. "We just haven't thought of it yet."

Chapter 13

"Let's look in the boxes," I suggest. "Maybe there's something we can use to escape."

The boxes are piled almost to the ceiling, and it's a problem just to get one open. Ariel is small and dexterous so we send her up like a mountain climber. She gains a foothold on each box and slowly makes her way to the top where she perches. Unfortunately since she is sitting on the box she can't open it.

"Can you reach the one next to you?" I call up. "Maybe you can open that one."

She looks around for a moment, and then calls down. "Miranda. There is something more interesting up here than the boxes."

"What?"

"An air vent in the ceiling."

"Really? Can you open it?"

"Let me see." She stands up slowly, reaches for the vent above her, and pulls. It comes away. She pulls herself up so her head is in the opening, then drops back onto the boxes.

"There is a long passage here," she says. "It has porous tiles all around."

"Big enough for a person?"

"Big enough for us," she says.

"Can you see where it goes?"

"No."

I look at Emma.

"Let's try it," she says. "The minute we go back into the hallway they'll catch us. And they're bound to check here soon and find us."

"Right. You go first. I'll catch you if you fall."

Emma slowly climbs up the boxes. Although she and I love to hike together I know she doesn't like steep drops. "Just don't look down," I encourage her.

She gets up with little trouble and helps boost Ariel into the overhead passage. I reach the top and boost Emma up. Then I pull myself up with Emma's help. The tiles lining the tunnel look like the kind we have in our music room at school — used to soundproof the room. With the extra crawl space lined with tiles, this office building would be completely soundproofed to the outside world. Why? I shudder as I think of the only logical explanation. Dr. Mullen's experiments — were there other clones that failed? And did they suffer? The sound of screaming babies would never leave these walls.

Ariel leads the way as we slither through the crawl space. Every little while there is another vent and we are able to look down and see what is happening. We reach a room where two people are working away at computers. No one is talking and there seems to be no concern about the three of us. In the next room, we can see the top of some huge vats. I hurry on, trying not to think about what they might be. Another room, and we see a few people in lab coats working with test tubes.

"We need to get back over the front corridor," I say, "so that we can get out the front door. They can't have locked that from the outside."

"Look," Ariel says, "I think that's where I was being kept."

I tell Ariel to move ahead a little and I peer down. It does look like the same room, screens and all.

"Let's go down here," I say. "We'll be close to the front door."

"But how?" says Emma, looking down. "No boxes."

"But there is a cot, right under the vent," I point out.

"Yeah," says Emma, "far under. Far enough

that we might not hit it, or hit it on the side, and break every bone in our bodies!"

"Let me go first," Ariel offers. "I can jump down easily, and then put some of the mattresses on top of each other for you two."

"Are you sure?" I ask.

"Yes," she answers. "I'm the smallest, it'll be easiest for me."

"All right," I agree.

I pull the grate off and push it aside. Ariel squeezes past us. Emma takes one arm, I take another, and we lower her down as far as we can.

"Now?" I say.

"Now," she replies.

Emma and I let go on the count of three. Ariel drops onto the cot. She scrambles up and grins at us. Then she runs to the other cots, pulls the mattresses off them and piles them onto the cot below us.

"All done," she calls.

"It still looks very far away," Emma groans.

"Any better idea?" I ask.

Emma shakes her head. "Let me go first and get it over with."

"No," I say, "let me. I've got a better chance than you of not getting hurt."

"Your superior physical abilities," Emma says.

"Not to mention all my dance training," I point out. "And then Ariel and I can catch you if necessary."

"All right," Emma agrees.

I grab the edges of the opening, hang for a minute, take a deep breath, then drop. I land hard on the cots and roll off, but get up basically unhurt.

"Come on, Emma," I call.

Ariel and I watch as she lowers herself, grabs on to the edge and quickly lets go. She falls slightly off the mattresses but I am there to catch her and push her back onto them.

"Whew!" she sighs as she scrambles off with my help.

"All right?" I ask.

"Yeah, okay."

I lead the way to the door, open it a crack and peek out. The big lug is walking down the corridor. I close the door.

"Not yet," I say. "We'd better wait. The big lug is out there."

"Big lug?" Ariel asks.

"Big guy? Very big?"

"I haven't seen him," Ariel says.

I turn to her. "Tell me what happened? How did they take you?"

"After you left me I went to my locker, and

you know, that's outside by the library. And while I was there Dr. Mullen came up to me. He said you had suddenly become ill and I needed to go with him. So I did. But he drove me here and put me in this room. He made me change my clothes and then he went away. When he came back he took me to a room that has lots of medical equipment. He took blood, did lots of tests and then just left me sitting here with nothing to read and no TV and nothing to do but worry and worry!"

"He substituted you," I tell her.

"What do you mean?"

"There's another clone. I've named her Eve. But she's pretending to be you. No wonder he had you switch clothes. He put her in the ones you were wearing so I wouldn't suspect anything."

"So no one would know I was missing." Ariel nods.

"I knew."

"How?"

"Because you are you. And she wasn't behaving like you."

This seems to interest Ariel. "How is she different?"

"Tell me why you are here," I say. "Do you know?"

"Not exactly," Ariel replies. "Except after Dr. Mullen did all those tests he said I was perfect. More perfect than you. More perfect than Eleven."

"That's Eve," I say.

"Probably," says Ariel. "I don't know if there are others. But I overheard him saying something about needing a prototype."

"So he really *is* going to make others," I say.

"But why?" Emma asks.

"Who knows," I grimace. "He's nuts. No doubt in his own mind he's got some great reason."

I open the door a crack and peek out.

"It's clear. Are you ready?"

"Let's go, then."

I open the door and lead the way, running full speed. We reach the door at the end of the corridor with no problem. I go to unlock it when suddenly a voice carries down the hallway.

"Not leaving so soon?"

I don't turn around. I am trying to turn the deadbolt and I do, but before I can even yank the door open, the big lug is there. He pushes me away from the door, and stands in front of it. Another very big man comes up beside him.

I whirl around. Dr. Mullen is walking toward us.

"Let us go!" I yell, although I know no one outside will hear me no matter how loud I shout.

"Calm down, my dear," he says. He reaches us and says, "Follow me."

The big guy gives us a shove. I look at Emma and Ariel. I see no alternative right now so I decide to go along with him. Well, what other choice is there?

We follow him into an office near the room from which we just escaped. He sits behind a desk, which looks similar to his desk at the clinic, covered in books and papers. There are three chairs already placed in front of the desk. Three? Was he expecting us? We sit.

"Ah, Miranda, I see you have noticed that I have three chairs waiting here." He picks up his notebook and scribbles in it. "Most interesting. You have been very useful to me today, thank you so much."

"What do you mean?" I ask.

"Do you really think I am stupid?" he asks.

"Yes," Emma smiles. I can see she doesn't want him to feel he's scaring us.

"Ah yes, Emma. You did spoil the experiment a little. I would have preferred to watch Ariel and Miranda on their own. Still, I think

I have an excellent idea of their reactions now, and I know what needs to be done."

"Could you speak in English, please?" I say, getting more and more angry, less and less afraid.

"But I am," he protests. "Don't you understand?" he asks. "Think."

I think. He says he is not as stupid as we think. And three chairs waiting. I gasp. "You knew we were following you? You knew we were here before I called home?"

"Good for you, Miranda," he says. "That is correct. This has all been an experiment. And you've been my little guinea pigs. I gave you the bait in my office, thinking you would have to try to find Ariel. But I wanted to be sure you would behave in the way I expected. And you did, right down to your escapade with the acid and your trek through the vents. Excellent."

Chapter 14

I just sit and stare at him. He knew everything?

"Look up," he says.

We do. I don't see anything but a ceiling.

"See that little clock on the wall?"

"Yes," I say.

"A camera," he beams. "Clever, what?"

"You've been watching us?" I say, incredulous.

"Oh, yes. Most certainly. From the start. Even before you came to my office. I thought it possible that when I took Ariel, you would notice. It would have been easier if you had not, of course. But once you did I wanted to know how much you would notice, how far you would go."

"Why?" Emma asks.

"Because," he smiles, "Ariel is a perfect prototype. *Physically*. But *emotionally*, well, that is harder to quantify. You showed some surprising characteristics when you discovered you were a clone, Miranda. Surprising. I need to know what other surprises you clones might have inside you. Stored away. Hidden. Yes, personality seems to be far less predictable."

"So let me get this straight," Emma says. "You knew we were following you. You let us in. You let us throw acid on that poor guy . . . you've followed our every move."

"Just a minute," I say. "That guy — his hands weren't bandaged."

"I didn't want you to hurt anyone," Mullen answers. "That was just foul-smelling water. But I was very interested in the fact that you were willing to do it. Very interested in that." He flips through his notebook and nods and clicks his tongue.

That makes me feel really sick.

"Why are you doing all this?" I demand. "It has to be more than just scientific curiosity. After all, you could always ask us to come in for tests, couldn't you? I'm sure you could have convinced my parents it was necessary for some reason."

"Clever, clever," he smiles. I wish I could wipe that smile off his face.

"You said prototype," I press on. "I think I should know if there are going to be more of me!"

"Here is the problem," he says. "You know in the movies where they say if I tell you, I'll have to kill you!"

All three of us squirm a little.

"Isn't it best if you don't know?" he asks.

"So does that mean you are going to let us go?" I ask.

"Oh, yes," he says. "Eventually. But I do think you need to calm down. If I let you go now you might run off to the police. I'm going to put you in a room for a little so that you can cool off and think. After all, if you go to the police everyone will know you are a clone."

"But what about Ariel?"

"She stays here."

"That won't do," I say.

"It will have to."

"Why? Tell me," I insist. "Whether I know or not, you'll still have Ariel. I'll still be tempted to go to the police. Maybe if I know why, I'll be less likely to go. My imagination might come up with something worse than what is actually happening."

He looks at me for a full minute, thinking.

"You are attached to Ariel, then?"

"No, I just came to rescue her for no reason."

"And do you not care about the one you call Eve? She is very ill."

"Of course I'm concerned about Eve."

"But not as much as Ariel."

"Well, no."

"Why?"

"Because I know Ariel better," I say, "obviously."

"Not obvious," he states. "If you were not so rebellious, you would only be thinking about what was presented to you. Why assume Eve is not Ariel? Especially when presented with evidence of a tumour?"

"Because," I say, frustrated, getting up from the chair. "I could tell it wasn't Ariel. And," I add, "I don't trust you!"

"That at least is logical," he comments. "Fine," he agrees. "I will let you in on my little scheme. I intend to produce babies. Perfect babies. You are aware no doubt that there is a huge demand for babies. I will supply that demand."

"For millions of bucks, no doubt," Emma scoffs.

"It is an expensive business," Dr. Mullen states. "I am only covering my costs. I do this as a scientific project first and foremost. As a humanitarian. But I need to do more work on the genes which control our emotions, our personalities."

"Babies who aren't any trouble?" I ask.

"That is correct."

"But," Ariel finally speaks up, "I *have* been trouble. So I am not perfect. Therefore you should let me go, too."

He beams at her. "Excellent reasoning, Ten," he says.

"Ariel," she corrects him.

"Ariel," he says. "But you are the most physically perfect specimen I have ever created. You will serve as the basis for all my new clones. Up until now, I had been using Miranda's DNA, but as you can see from Eve, it is not going as planned."

This gives me pause. What's wrong with my DNA? Is it defective in some way?

Dr. Mullen continues speaking to Ariel. "From now on I will use only your DNA."

"You will experiment on me?"

"Don't worry," he says gently. "I'd never hurt you. And in a way, you can think of yourself as mother to all the new clones that come out of our work."

"Not very original," I say, trying to needle him. "Every movie you see on TV has a mad scientist cloning babies for sale."

"That is because it's the logical next step, isn't it?" he says. "Mass culture is often very accurate about where the world is heading." He rises from his chair. "Now, girls, it's time for you to go to your room. I believe you know the way. I'll send in dinner."

"Our families will start to worry soon," I warn him.

"Oh, no," he corrects me. "Eve — who sounds just like you, Miranda — has left a message for Emma's parents saying Emma is at your house. And she's told your parents, Miranda, that you called to say you were staying at Emma's. I think we have a little time for you to think about what to do. Think carefully."

"We can't talk privately if we are being watched," I object.

"Ah, the camera. I'll turn it off."

"Why should we believe you?" I scoff.

"Come with me. I'll show you."

We follow him. He leads us to one of the first rooms we looked in, full of computers. He shows us the screen, which displays the room with the cots. They are still piled high.

"You will have to clean up your mess," he comments. I don't bother to answer. He's worried about a mess?

He flips a switch and the picture goes off.

"As soon as we're gone you'll put it back on," I point out.

"There is a tiny green light on the second hand," he says. "If it is on," and he points to a matching clock on the wall behind him, "you are being watched." He throws another switch. I see the light go off. "When it is off, the camera is off, too.

"Ariel," he orders. "Show your friends to your room."

Ariel leads the way. We get to the room and I check the clock. Green light off.

"I suppose we can talk," I say. "But I suggest we talk quietly. He may have microphones hidden, who knows?"

"Who knows anything?" Emma sighs. "He says we're free to go. What if he only wants to see what decision we'll make? What if this is still part of the experiment? What if we are never getting out of here?"

I stare at her.

She's right. This could all be part of his little plot. In which case we are truly in danger for our lives.

Chapter 15

"Selling perfect babies," I mutter as we sit on the cot. "And all little Ariels. Imagine."

"We have to decide what to do," Emma says.

"We can't just leave Ariel and pretend nothing has happened," I say. "That's out of the question."

"You must," Ariel states.

"Why?" I ask.

"Because if you don't, it's possible we'll *all* die," she points out. "He's giving you a chance to live. You have to take it. It's only logical."

"I don't care if it's logical. I hate it and I'm not doing it! I can't leave you behind and pretend Eve is the real you."

"I think we should try to escape again," Emma suggests, getting up and pacing. "I can't stand the thought of him getting away with all of this."

"But at least no one will die," Ariel points out. "He doesn't want to hurt us. He's a scientist. He values us."

"Only as experiments," I remind her. Then I remember that he practically brought up Ariel. The only father she's ever known. That's a creepy thought.

"What if we don't agree?" I asked. "What do you think he'll do?"

"The logical thing," she answers, "is to kill all of us. That will leave no one to tell on him. He can take my DNA and create new ones after we're gone. Actually it's quite kind of him *not* to kill us. It would be easier and more logical to do so."

She's talking like we have no choice. But there is always a choice — of some sort.

The door opens and a young woman comes in, followed by the big lug. She is carrying a tray filled with hamburgers, fries and Cokes. When I smell that familiar greasy scent I realize that I'm starving. She puts it down on a table and leaves. It does flash through my mind that if he wants to drug us and then kill us the food would be a way to go. I notice Emma looking at it suspiciously, too. As if reading our thoughts Ariel says, "He has never tried to trick me with the food. It's probably safe." She grabs a burger and starts to eat. After a minute Emma and I join her.

But after we've eaten we know we have to make a decision. And I just don't know what to do — I'm not willing to go along with Dr. Mullen. I *have* to think of something else.

Just then the door opens and, well, I would say Ariel walks in. But it couldn't be Ariel, because she is sitting on her cot. Could it be another clone?

The girl closes the door behind her. Ariel is staring at her. They are exact doubles. Then I recognize the outfit she is wearing.

"Eve?"

"Hello, Miranda."

"Eve! How on earth did you get here?"

"I used to live here," she says, calmly. "And when you said you were in trouble, in a lab, I decided you must be here."

"How did you get here, though?"

"I hid in Dr. Mullen's van," she says, very matter-of-fact.

"You did *what*?" I can't believe my ears.

"And when he had been stopped for a few minutes, I got out. I waited until Bob went outside to smoke. Then I walked in. I did not hurry. People are used to seeing me here."

"But they think you are me," Ariel says. "I'm the one they think lives here now."

"I want to help you to escape," Eve says.

"Eve, that's wonderful," I say, "but we can't put you in danger."

"What danger?" says Eve. "I do not mind

being here. I miss it. It is my home."

"Is this the place you were homesick for?" I ask.

"Yes."

"But wouldn't you rather be with us, in a real home?"

"I do not know," Eve answers. "I am not used to your home. I have to pretend. And I am not very good at it. I do not know how to be Ariel." She pauses. "I watched carefully at the drama class to see if I could learn how to pretend but I was not able to fool you," she says.

And then, suddenly, I have an idea. "Oh! Oh! Oh!" I exclaim.

Emma looks at me hopefully. "You've had a brainwave!"

"Yes. Yes. What if Eve does stay? Only she pretends to be Ariel? And Ariel pretends to be Eve? Wanna bet Dr. Mullen saw Eve come in on the cameras? He probably knows she's here." I look at Ariel. "Do you think you could pull it off?"

"Pretend to be Eve?" she says. "I don't know. I've never met Eve, remember."

She's right. I draw them together. "Eve, meet Ariel. Ariel, meet Eve."

Ariel smiles at Eve. Eve looks solemnly at Ariel.

"But Eve," I say, "if you agree with my plan, you'd have to stay here."

"I am dying," she says simply. "I wish to do that where things are . . . familiar."

"But you would have to pretend to be Ariel," I caution, "and you weren't too good at it before."

"I can tell her what to do," Ariel offers.

I look at Emma and draw her aside. "What do you think?" I ask. "Would it be awful to leave her here?"

"Not if she wants to be here. We can try to come back for her later," Emma suggests. "And let's face it, it might be our only chance."

I think. I have to take care of Emma too. I can't be responsible for Dr. Mullen killing her.

"All right," I say, turning back to them. "Let's do it. First you have to change clothes."

I look up at the camera to be sure it is still off. It seems to be, so the girls quickly switch clothes. Ariel has her long hair pulled back in a ponytail, Eve is wearing hers straight. Ariel gives Eve her scrunchy and Eve pulls her hair back.

"Now," I say, "I'm going to ask Ariel a question. Eve, you listen. Ariel, how do you feel about this decision?"

"Okay, I'm not crazy about it because I really liked being with Miranda and going to school and all that, but it's logical so we have to do it." Ariel answers. Eve mimics her, just like in the mirror exercise.

I turn to Eve. "Eve, why did you hide in my van?"

"I am made for Miranda. She said she was in trouble. I must help her."

Ariel copies her.

Soon Ariel realizes that she just needs to remember the way she spoke before she began living with me. It's easier for her. Eve has the more difficult task.

"Remember," I say to Eve, "how we had to pretend to be characters in that acting class?"

"Yes," she replies.

"Well, just pretend the same way. And don't worry. Ariel is upset now, so she's not happy the way she was at home. Use contractions, like can't instead of cannot. And sometimes try to be a little cranky or not nice."

"I'm nice!" Ariel objects.

"But you've learned to think for yourself," I say. "And that's an important part of Ariel."

"He will discover I am Eve soon," Eve says. "When I get sick again."

The door opens.

"Ah, Number Eleven, I saw you come in." Dr. Mullen says as he walks into the room.

I knew it. He must watch everything. But he is talking to Ariel, not Eve. So far it's working.

He speaks sternly. "You should not have come back. I told you what you had to do."

"But I cannot pretend well," Ariel says, pretending to be Eve. "I could not fool Miranda."

"You do not need to fool Miranda," he points out. "You only need to fool her parents. And they are convinced you are Ten." He turns to us. "Well, what is the decision then?"

I step forward. "I think you are horrible," I say. "Really horrible. But we can't think of any way out of here unless you let us out. And I can't be responsible for you hurting Emma. Or Ariel. So we've decided to leave Ariel behind. She says she'll do it. She doesn't want us to be hurt."

"Of course she doesn't," he says. "Of course not. She was brought up to serve you. To give up her life for you. But she doesn't have to die now. She'll be a valuable prototype. And we'll all be happy."

"What about Eve?" I say. "Can't you do *anything* for her?"

"I'm afraid not," he replies. "Well, time to get you girls home. Let's put those bikes in my car and I'll drop you at Emma's house. Ten, you come with me."

Before I can stop her, Ariel turns. Reflex action, I suppose. But then Eve, who is supposed to go with him, says, "He said Ten! Not Eleven. Honestly!" And she turns to me, talking very fast, just like Ariel. "Goodbye, sis. It was great while it lasted. I had lots of fun. I'll, I'll always remember you . . . " And she throws her arms around me. I can feel her tears on my cheeks. They are real tears, not fake. And I suddenly wonder if she was pretending when she was talking to me — convincing me she'd rather be here than at home with me so that she could save us. She pulls away, and then hugs Emma too. "Bye, Emma." She looks at Ariel. "Goodbye, Eve," she says.

"I'll be back for you girls in a minute," Dr. Mullen says.

They leave. We stand there. Fearful of talking, afraid we've been discovered. Time goes by slowly; every second seems like hours.

But Dr. Mullen returns about ten minutes later without Eve. He leads us down the hall and out the front door.

It is dark. The sky is clear and full of stars.

The air smells so sweet. I take a deep breath and realize how close I came to never taking another one. We get into the van. I'm still not sure I can trust the good doctor, but within fifteen minutes we are at Emma's house unloading the bikes.

"Remember," Dr. Mullen says. "Tell no one. If you do I cannot guarantee Ariel's safety. Or any of yours." And he drives off, leaving us standing outside the house.

Chapter 16

The three of us hurry into the house. Emma's parents run over to us, frantic. Emma's mom says, "Where have you girls been? Miranda's mother called because she couldn't find Ariel and was worried, thought maybe she'd come here. And I told her you girls were at her house and she said no, you were here, and we've all been worried sick!"

She pauses to catch her breath. Emma's dad is standing just behind her. He's got a temper, and I can see he isn't pleased. Actually they both have tempers. But at least you know where you stand with them. Unlike my parents, who are always calm, except it turns out they are lying to you half the time.

Emma is obviously at a loss for words. What do we do? I decide we need to tell someone. They already know about me and about Dr. Mullen.

"We need to tell them, Emma," I say.

"What about Eve?" she replies.

"This might be her only chance," I reply.

Ariel stands quietly for once. This entire episode seems to have taken the sparkle out of her eyes.

"Tell us what?" asks Emma's dad, suddenly more concerned than angry.

"Come on," her mom says, "and sit down. Anyone want something to drink?" She gives us juice. While waiting for the kettle to boil so she can make tea, she calls my parents, assures them we're all right, and suggests we stay the night as it's awfully late to drive all that way.

When we're all settled in at the kitchen table, I tell them what's happened. I try to shorten it, but it's at least an hour before I'm finished and they've asked all their questions.

"He has to be stopped," Dr. Green says.

"But how? If we call the police, everyone will know about Miranda and Ariel," Emma objects. "Their lives wouldn't be worth living — TV cameras around them every single second. It would be horrible."

"Let me think." Dr. Green says. "Wait a minute." He looks at Mrs. Green. "The security guards at the clinic? I hand-picked them. They're tough and loyal to me."

Mrs. Green nods. Dr. Green motions for us

to leave the room while he makes his calls.

The three of us flop down in the living room. I obviously crash right out because the next thing I know Mrs. Green is waking me up. Ariel and Emma are just waking up too.

"Girls," she says, "it's almost midnight. Dr. Green is going with the guards over to the lab. We need to know where it is."

Emma opens her mouth when I interrupt. "I'm not sure, are you, Emma? I'd have to go," I say. "I could show them."

"I'm sure if you describe the streets they can find it." Mrs. Green says firmly. "There's no need for you girls to go."

"But we want to, Mom!" Emma objects. "Eve is there, and that horrible Dr. Mullen is so creepy. I want to make sure they've got him. Besides, Eve doesn't know Dad. She'll be scared."

Mrs. Green goes out and then comes back in a few minutes. "You can go over there in your dad's car," she says, although she doesn't look thrilled about it.

We scramble up and get ready to go, first telling the guards — who are waiting in the kitchen and who are even bigger than Bob and his pal — where the lab is. Emma grabs us all jackets. It feels cool out now, even though it was so hot earlier.

We pile into Dr. Green's car, Emma in front, Ariel and me in the back. I go from being tired to being wired with nervous energy.

We drive through the night and it is completely quiet in the car. It reminds me of that first night trip I took with my mother to the clinic — was it only a few months ago now? My eyesight had gone and I was going to be checked in. I was afraid I was about to die.

But maybe death isn't the worst thing in the world. Back then I didn't know what I really had to be afraid of. I would find out that I was a clone. I would find out that my parents, whom I loved, were willing to do anything to cheat death. And it would force me to think about who I am.

I look at Ariel sitting beside me. She is staring out the window. I wonder if she is thinking the same thing: Who are we really? Am I just a carbon copy of the original Jessica? Do I have my own personality or am I just preprogrammed by my genes to react a certain way? Emma says we are all programmed in a way. And if that is true, then what makes us unique is maybe pushing against that, testing that, trying to figure out what is programmed and what it really means to think for ourselves.

Ariel takes my hand. "I'm scared," she whispers.

"Why?"

"If Eve and I can just be switched, what does it matter if I'm here or if she's here?"

So she *has* been thinking similar thoughts. And doesn't that prove what she just said? We are so much alike, engineered to be the same, that we even think the same. Maybe there is no point.

Dr. Green speaks. "I couldn't help but overhear Ariel," he says. "May I suggest something?"

"Yes," she says.

"You have a soul," he says. "That's unique to you. You and Eve and Miranda are all different. You'll make different choices in your lives. Maybe when you look at those choices you won't like some of them. So you'll change. Life is complicated.

"Ariel," he adds, "it isn't easy growing up. Even if you aren't a clone! Right, Emma?"

"Yeah," Emma says. "That's for sure."

"Let me tell you a little secret," he continues. "Life isn't that easy when you're an adult either."

We turn into the drive that leads to the secret lab. My heart is in my throat. What if Dr. Mullen found out about Eve after we left?

What would he do to her? Did we make the right choice? It seemed we did at the time, but maybe I was just looking for an easy way to save my skin.

The cars pull up to the front door. We watch as the two guards go to the front door. Much to my surprise, they seem to go into the building right away. I wait. Will Dr. Mullen try to escape? What will happen?

Finally I see the men come out. No one is with them. I can't stand it. I get out of the car.

"Miranda!" Dr. Green warns me, but then he gets out too. One of the guards comes toward us.

"What's happening?" Dr. Green says.

"I don't know," the guard answers. "There's nobody there. The whole place is empty."

I am so stunned I can't speak for a moment. "It can't be!" I exclaim. And then I'm running. Emma and Ariel are right behind me. We burst through the open door. I open the first door, to the room that had all the computers in it. Empty! We race from room to room finding the same thing in each one — nothing! The cots are still in the room we were held in, but all the equipment, computers, people, are gone.

The three of us stop finally, out of breath.

"He must have known we'd go to your father," I say to Emma. "I don't know how your father can say Ariel and I are individuals," I add, disgusted. "Dr. Mullen knew exactly what we'd do! And he should. He made us!"

I sink down on the floor, head in my hands. "Poor Eve. He'll find out soon. And he'll be really mad."

Emma sits beside me. "He knew you'd tell, not because he made you but because he knows you are a good person. And that you're even more worried about Eve than about your own safety."

"But do you think we'll be safe?" Ariel asks. "Maybe he'll be mad at us. Maybe he's watching us right now." She looks up at the camera on the wall.

I get a chill down my spine.

"He could be," I say.

"Ugh," Emma grimaces.

We hurry outside. "What if Ariel is right?" I say, once outside. "He'll know now for sure about Eve."

"He's probably too busy getting out of town to be keeping tabs on us right now," Emma says.

"Come on, girls," Dr. Green calls. "Time to go. There's nothing left for us to do here."

I put one arm around Emma and the other around Ariel and we walk back to the car together. It's all over — for now.

Chapter 17

I am sitting in bed thinking about Eve, because it is exactly a month since she and Dr. Mullen disappeared. I stare out the window. The sun is shining, as usual, and Ariel is sound asleep, the cool morning breeze making the drapes billow just over her bed. The phone rings and I jump.

"Hello?"

"Miranda?"

It's Eve! "Eve!"

"Yes, yes, it is me!"

"I was just thinking about you!"

"I know. Because it is a month ago exactly that Dr. Mullen took me. I have been planning to call you today. But I only have a minute. It was complicated to arrange this." She hurries on. "I know you must be worried about me. But when Dr. Mullen found out it was really me and not Ariel, he vowed to cure me so he could use me as his prototype. I don't know whether he can or not, but he seems to think it is not so difficult. He will not be able to use my DNA, as he would have done with Ariel, but I will serve as a model for his clients. I cannot make him angry, though. He is my one chance." She pauses. "I miss you."

"I miss you too," I say, fervently. "But I am so glad you are alive."

"Dr. Mullen saved enough of Ariel's DNA so he can carry on with his experiments. And he is showing me off to many strangers."

"But how is your health?"

"Will I live, do you mean?"

"Yes, yes."

"I do not know, but I am on a new drug and I will soon have surgery and he says we will know in a month or two."

"Will you call? I want to help get you back."

"I will try. Now I have to go."

"Wait, wait!" I try to think. "Where are you?"

"If I tell you, I know you will put yourself in danger."

I hear something. It sounds like a foghorn. "Are you by the ocean?"

"Miranda, I have to go."

"Come home," I say.

"I'll try." The line goes dead.

Ariel is sitting up in bed. "That was Eve, wasn't it?"

"How did you know?"

"I could tell from what you were saying. She's alive!"

I nod.

"What did she say?"

Ariel comes over and sits on my bed. By all rights she should be in her own room, but she says she gets lonely in there and half the time she sleeps in here with me.

"She sounded all right," I say. "She thinks Dr. Mullen might be able to cure her. He's trying. And he saved your DNA and is using it."

"To make his perfect babies," she says.

"Apparently."

We sit for a moment. I'm just glad Eve is alive. I thought she might be dead. I've cried many nights. I've worried about my decision. I've wondered if I didn't take the easy way out, the end justifying the means. I've wondered if Dr. Mullen has somehow programmed that into me. Maybe my so-called goodness was only wanting to be good because it produced the desired result, peace with my parents and teachers.

What does it mean to act with goodness, for the right reasons, without thinking about the result? But we never know what the result of our actions will be. I was sure Dr.

Mullen would let Eve die. Instead the opposite is true. I suppose the only thing I know for sure is what Dr. Green said. Life is complicated.

"What are you thinking?" Ariel says.

"A bunch of stuff," I reply.

I don't like to talk to her about all of this because I don't want her to feel any of it is her fault. It isn't! And she has enough to get used to. We're on holiday now, school over, so we're home more and Mother and Father have to deal with her more. In a way it's almost funny because she's not at all the goody-goody I used to be. Yesterday she went out with Jen and came home two hours late and was hardly sorry or worried or anything! I wouldn't have dreamed of doing anything like that.

Of course, Mother and Father are still recovering from the news that I was right about Eve and Dr. Mullen. I'm *pretty* sure they didn't have anything to do with his nefarious plans. Pretty sure, but not one hundred percent positive. I mean if they can lie that way once — the way they did to me, letting me think I was a normal kid — they can certainly lie again.

Father keeps taking me out to dinner so we can talk "one on one," and I listen. He assures me that I can trust them. I'm just keeping my options open.

"I'm glad Dr. Mullen is taking care of her," Ariel sighs. "I only wish she was free. Not his . . . "

"His lab rat," I finish for her.

"Isn't there a way we could find her?" Ariel asks.

"You'd think there would be," I reply. "Let's think about it. And talk to Emma."

"We'll see her at acting school today," Ariel reminds me.

"I know," I say.

Ariel is taking a class for younger kids at the same time as my class. And Mother drives us. When I told them about Eve I also told them about our class. I don't want to live surrounded by lies anymore. They gave in, but it was funny as they tried to tell me I shouldn't lie to them. Funny in a weird way, not a laugh-out-loud way.

"Want to go for a swim?" Ariel asks. She looks at me hopefully. I have to smile back. Since I've got her back I don't get mad with her as easily. I'm just glad she's here safe and sound. And since I've lost Mother and Father as family I can trust, at least I have her. We've become pretty close.

I get up and look for my swimsuit.

"What are you thinking now?" Ariel says.

"I'm wondering what else Dr. Mullen is up to," I reply.

She looks at me.

"I wonder, too."

CAROL MATAS is the author of many books for children and young adults, in a variety of genres. She is best known for her historical novels, including *The War Within, Rebecca, After the War, Lisa* and *Daniel's Story. The Second Clone* is the sequel to the best-selling contemporary thriller *Cloning Miranda.* Carol also writes fantasy novels in collaboration with Perry Nodelman.

Carol has received many honours for her work, including the Silver Birch Award, the Jewish Book Prize and two nominations for the Governor General's Award. She lives in Winnipeg, Manitoba.